BENEVOLENCE

PATRICIA CRUMPLER

World Castle Publishing, LLC
Pensacola, Florida
Copyright © Patricia Crumpler 2021
Hardback ISBN: 9798757898599
Paperback ISBN: 9781956788228
eBook ISBN: 9781956788235
First Edition World Castle Publishing, LLC, November 15, 2021
http://www.worldcastlepublishing.com
Licensing Notes
Cover: Karen Fuller

DEDICATION

Thanks to Robert Heinlein, Edgar Rice
Burroughs, James Gunn, and all the other
twentieth century
sci-fi authors who fired my imagination.

ONE

"All rise."

Arlen Rowell had heard the bailiff's directive before. Now he and other convicted prisoners awaited their sentencing, conveniently done en masse.

With narrowed eyes, the judge sent his contempt to the six men and one woman who stood before him. "Killers, all," he snarled, "but I'm about to give you another swing at the piñata, not for treats, for years."

Silently the courtroom waited for the judge's next words. "Instead of what you deserve, death by brain shut-down, I'm offering you life."

The courtroom buzzed. The judge held up his hand. "Not a good life. In fact, some of you may prefer your easy death." A light murmur began, then died away to hear the terms. "You will be sent to serve aboard one of the Interstellar Havens for Plague Victims...."

The woman prisoner took a step forward. "Freak Ships? Pass. Kill me."

Such was the reputation of the Freak Ships.

The buzz escalated into a roar. The judge's raised hand took time to quiet the noise. "Those of you who want to live," he indicated a woman standing next to an antechamber door, "follow her."

The woman's pointed features resembled the rats Arlen trapped in his store's basement. Unlike the painless death of the rodent box, where a quick dose of gas eliminated the creature, this woman looked as if she were about to be cornered, ready to bite.

Arlen and three other men followed rat-lady. As they left the courtroom, the judge sentenced the remaining prisoners who elected death over life on the ships—the huge crafts holding the survivors of the Fall-Out Plague.

Inside the antechamber, the woman nodded

to a guard who shut the door. She glared at the men. "Sit. I'm Loren Drutz, Assistant to the Secretary of Humane Welfare. It's my unpleasant duty to be in charge of the...."

The man next to Arlen finished her sentence. "Freak Ships."

Loren Drutz scowled. "When you get to your ships, you can call them whatever you wish. No one will know; no one will care. For the record, your names will appear on the executed list. You will never return to Earth." She smirked. "And I doubt you'll ever set foot on any other planet. You will become the ship's single Normal human, the Liaison."

The guard thudded a valise on the table and opened it.

Loren Drutz removed four black notebooks and pitched them to each prisoner. "Once you've left Earth, your only Normal contact will be a space clerk, the unlucky fellow who takes your reports in person." She tapped the valise. "The only communication allowed from the ships is the six-month visit from the clerk. The ship bringing him does not get close. The Humane Welfare clerk flies a capsule, which docks at a special airlock to meet you. As the sole Normal aboard the ships, you, and you alone, can interact with him. Between reports, believe me, the clerk will do his best to forget you, the craft, and the…." She shuddered.

Another man at the table said, "Freaks."

Loren Drutz snarled, "Plague Survivors."

The same man held up his hand. "I have questions."

The corner of Drutz's lip curled. "No, you don't. Everything you need to know is in that notebook." She snapped the valise shut and headed toward the door. With her back to them, she tossed her words to the guard. "They're all yours."

The guard pushed a rear door opening into a dark tunnel. "Come with me." He ushered them into the shadowy space. A whoosh heralded an air shuttle that stopped without sound. They all boarded. The smooth ride through the dimness lasted a few minutes.

No one spoke, giving Arlen a chance to think about what he'd agreed to. What other choice could he make? He'd never see his family again with either decision, but at least he'd duck the death penalty. He wasn't even thirty, and he wanted to live. Live for what? Freaks? He'd missed the chance to square things with his father. He'd never given the man a single opportunity to feel proud. So, life on the mutant ships or death. What did it matter?

Everyone knew about the Freak Ships, but no one mentioned them, as if thinking about the victims of the Fall-Out Plague might bring the curse to you. Perhaps data existed regarding how many people had perished and how many survived, but it was history, a past well worth forgetting. The government had done a good job helping people forget.

The craft came to an easy stop, and the guard cleared his throat. "We'll wait in that room over there," he indicated a round chamber a few feet away from the shuttle. "It's a subterranean room under the rocket port."

The guard sat down in one of the seats rimming the room. He offered no other explanation.

An underground chamber? For people

like us? Arlen had not become accustomed to the treatment of criminals. It had all gone so fast. The break-in of his store, the confrontation of the robber. His small grocery store had done well, made money, and filled a need in that neighborhood. The late hours paid off until the drunken son of the Fire Chief tried his hand at robbery. Arlen tackled the mature teen who pointed a gun that went off during the fight and killed the young man. Arlen's security camera had caught it all on tape, enough visual evidence to clear him. Curiously, the tape was lost before the trial. The bereaved Chief and his wife wanted "closure," they said. Their son was no robber, just a kid wanting a candy bar on his way home. Arlen had been railroaded to protect the reputation of the city official.

He looked around him. Although he didn't know the story of the other three prisoners, they would be thinking about their decision to live as well. Would one of them regret having a fistfight with his father? Had any one of them let pride keep him from making amends before his old man died? Or, was any other man, innocent of a convicted crime, be guilty of not doing one single thing to make his father proud?

The drips of the leaky water fountain echoed in the chamber as each man kept to himself. Arlen hated the quiet moments; they allowed too much time for remorse, and he had experienced a lot of them in the past weeks.

The sound of the keyed entry preceded the open door. "Let's go," a new guard said. They rode a dingy elevator upwards. Rocket ports were known for their elegant designs, but like life, the ports had their dark side, the hidden underbelly, places good citizens didn't know about and wouldn't want to.

The elevator jerked to a stop. "This is the hold of the rocket," the guard said. Arlen had been on rockets before but didn't know the hold had seats — with chains.

Inside, the guard tapped a narrow metal door. "Pee now."

They took turns using the room and were shackled afterwards. Each seat had a single bottle of water. The guard checked the chains and left.

Arlen drank his water. Soon after take-off,

the rocket's pressurized gasses would induce sleep for the faster-than-light journey. He wondered where they were going and how long it would take. The noise from the engines deafened him. Sleep couldn't come soon enough. During the gas-induced sleep, he dreamed of his father, a common theme. He heard the shouts of the argument and telling Dad to shove the Water Filtration business up his ass. He rewound the tape of him stomping out of the house, ready to take on the world — by himself. The emotions nearly overwhelmed him, not the least being regret.

When he awoke, the short blasts of the rockets meant the ship was maneuvering into port. Which port? Arlen had enjoyed his prior rocket trips. He paid extra for a port so he could see the planet from orbit, watch the landing, and admire the pilot's skill as the vessel lowered into the concave cradle. He would marvel when the stilts unfolded like a ballet dancer to stabilize the craft. There were no windows in this part of the ship. He wouldn't get the landing show. Only the soft bump of the pad meant they were setting down.

Arlen eyed the narrow metal door and squirmed. Probably a twenty-four-hour flight, by his urgent need to pee. Most likely, the passengers would disembark before the men in the hold were taken away. The interminable wait became more of an emergency, but the other men were eyeing the same door. He relaxed; what else could he do?

Finally, two men in air police uniforms unshackled the first prisoner, who headed for the toilet. One by one, they were freed from the chains. They walked single file, with an air cop at both ends of the line. The dark and dusty hallways weren't part of the fancy rocket ports above them. They came to a stop at a hub, a junction of multiple tunnels. After a short wait, each man was escorted by two air cops who took them in different directions.

Arlen's quiet demeanor, his post FTL lag, and the depression regarding his future stifled conversation with his attendants. They stopped at a small office where one cop rang the bell.

A small man, bathed in unhappiness, answered. An engraved sign on his desk said "E. Blake." He gave Arlen the once-over. "You're the

Normal for the Freak Ship, I assume. No, don't talk; just listen. We're leaving immediately on a transit ship, headed for the Benevolence." He shook his head and gave a cold laugh. "Benevolence, my ass. If it was up to me…." Blake pulled the trigger on an invisible gun.

Arlen cleared his throat to speak.

"No talking. I'll tell you what you need to know, which is when we get to the Freak Ship, I'll take the remains of the former Liaison, and you will take his place."

"Wait," Arlen said.

The man ripped open his desk drawer, pulled out an injection unit, and slammed its needle into Arlen's arm through his prison overalls.

Nausea waved through Arlen's body, and the last thing he heard was Blake saying, "I told you not to talk."

TWO

Arlen's head still swam when Blake shook him awake.

"Get up. We're almost there. Your new home."

Blake's mocking happiness added a new ripple of pain, pounding Arlen's forehead.

Arlen stood, grabbing a metal conduit along the wall to stabilize. "Where..."

Blake, a good six inches shorter, shoved Arlen toward a closed oval portal studded with round heads. "We're about to board the capsule. It's a one-man capsule, so you'll be against the wall behind my seat. Too bad you're large."

With a soft metallic rasp, the sides of the oval separated, showing the interior of a small egg-shaped craft. A single padded chair sat in front of a dashboard where lights produced flickering images on controls.

"Find a place behind the chair," Blake said, pushing Arlen toward the door.

Arlen turned, ready to slam the bozo against the nearest wall. Four armed guards raised their lasers. He nodded and tolerated Blake's next shove.

The gap behind the seat couldn't accommodate his height, nor was there room for him to lie down. He ducked the ceiling and squeezed in. After a few positionings, he folded his knees up and wrapped his hands around his lower legs. "Let this be a short ride," he said quietly. A windshield over the dash provided a vista of black, sparkling with myriad twinklers. "Space," he said in a soft breath.

Blake took his seat and flicked a lever. "Shut up."

Grating sounds and a brief rocking meant the capsule had left the ship. Arlen forgot his discomfort for the moment and invited the thrill of the vast universe to restore him. He strained his neck to see both sides of the view, trying to ignore Blake's head blocking the ebony space-scape. The beautiful scene did not completely distract him from his discomfort. His aching butt made him brutally aware of the pressing bones, and soon his calves began to cramp. Vigorous rubbing helped; however, the sight of a silvery ship, looking like a shining bean at that distance completely distracted him. Arlen kept his eye on Benevolence until it loomed massively over them, like a pea against a football.

Blake folded his arms and let the auto-docker mate with the mammoth craft. Things clanked, clicked, and coupled, making the capsule and the great ship one unit.

When Blake hit a red button, the capsule door opened onto shiny metal. "Before I open the Freak Ship door, I'm having disinfectant spray fumigate the airlock. When I tell you, step into that room. Don't leave the entry chamber into the living area until I shut the capsule door. In twenty minutes, you will bring the remains of uh...the other Liaison, the rich guy...." Blake rubbed his fingers and thumb together, the sign for bribery.

He sneered. "Whatever his name was. If you aren't back when I open the capsule door, then I have met my requirements, and I can leave this nightmare." He grimaced, adding, "I'm an honorable man in service to my country. I'm bound to do my duty. For twenty minutes."

"Honorable service," Arlen muttered. Right. He stood, unfolded, and, massaging his leg muscles, waited for the signal to enter.

"Here," Blake smacked Arlen's chest with the black notebook. "This is yours." He chuckled a sinister snort. "Don't say Humane Welfare never gave you nothing." The ship's gleaming portal parted. "Go."

Arlen entered the docking room, the airlock of the Benevolence. The ship's sleek door slid closed on the capsule. Disinfectant stung his nose. He coughed.

Alone in the small entry chamber, Arlen could barely gather his thoughts. Where would he find the body of the previous Liaison? What did the guy die from? He walked forward and patted the wall to find controls. His hand skimmed over a bar. Pressed, it gave way, parting a section of the wall. He walked through.

Light, as bright as noon, assaulted his eyes. Stepping to a metal sidewalk, Arlen took in the view. A high dome, painted blue like the sky, silhouetted three and four-story buildings. Structures situated in grids sat across each other, divided by dark metallic streets. It looked like a city. In the distance, he saw people. They looked like people, but not quite. He leaned against what appeared to be a light pole to watch. A woman with hair on one side of her head passed by him. She turned the hairless side toward him as she passed to better stare at his rumpled orange jumpsuit—the prison garb. Did they have prisons here? He knew so little about the Freak Ships. Why didn't the people of Earth know more about the ones who lived on the Interstellar Havens?

Three young women chatted as they passed him. Arlen pulled back from them. The girl in the middle had things jutting out of her face. He barely noticed the deformities of the others. A man came from the other direction with mottled skin patched in blue, black, and beige. A large egg shape protruded from his forehead.

Arlen's stomach turned as he watched the man approach. Realizing he needed help, he forced himself to stop the man. "Excuse me. I'm new here."

The man eyed Arlen's orange jumpsuit. "New?"

Swallowing hard, Arlen groped for words. "I'd like to find the Liaison. Do you know anything about that?"

"I don't know for sure. Check his office where he killed himself. The staff is still there, I think."

"Where would that be?"

"You must be the new Liaison. See that three-story building three streets south?" He chuckled. "We have our own directional system. That's north." The bluish man pointed in the opposite direction. "That's south, see? Go to that place. Top floor."

Arlen nodded. "Thanks." He headed south, looking side to side, taking in the place that would be home.

Although most of the interior of the great ship was metal, plants grew in any space large enough to have enough soil to hold them. Soil? He had so many questions. A short walk took him to the three-story building, where an exterior elevator brought him to the top floor. Across the hall from the landing, a sign said "Liaison Office." With trepidation, Arlen opened the door. Excepting the furniture, the room, one office and four cubicles, was empty. The door with a glass panel reading "Liaison Officer" sat ajar. He entered. A small box sat atop a wooden desk. Words in hand-written letters on the box said, "Rest In Peace, Mr. Thaler."

Arlen ran his finger over the box and bit his lip.

"Hello," a woman's voice said. "I'll bet you're the new Liaison Officer."

He took a breath, wondering what he would find attached to that voice. Summoning his courage, he turned. Tall, robust, the honey blonde stretched her mouth apart in a grotesque smile. A smile showing teeth but no lips.

The lipless slit turned down into a frown. "You might get used to it. Mr. Thaler couldn't. Poor guy. He came here because he insulted a diplomat's wife. It doesn't pay to piss Earth people off." She took a step closer. "We had him cremated, and we prayed over the ashes. It's the best we could do. He was a good guy. Not like he could affect any major changes for us, but he tried. The Normals they send are persona non grata."

Arlen nodded. "I need to get this to Blake."

"The H. W. clerk."

"Such a guy," Arlen sneered.

"Mr. Thaler didn't think much of him. By the way, I'm Samantha, Mr. Thaler's assistant. The other staff and I just came back from the morning break wagon."

Arlen could not take his eyes from her face. A pleasant face, soft eyes, chiseled nose, she was lovely until he saw the bottom third, where her straight white teeth took center stage. She had no lips; a mouth slit gaped open, showing her teeth at all times.

"I know," She dropped her gaze and sighed. "It's gross. If you can't stand to look at me... There are other people who can take over my job. Some of us can cover their, uhm, mutations."

Had she seen something in his expression? A wave of regret choked him. "No. I, I, uh, you're fine." He grabbed the box. "I need to be at the portal right away. Uhm, I'll be back."

Arlen ran to the elevator, fidgeting while it made its way down. Taking his bearing, he hurried to the light post he'd seen when he emerged from the entry chamber. Panicked, he searched the area for a handle. He noticed a button on a panel and pressed it. The portal opened into the small room, the smell of disinfectant still present. As his eyes adjusted to the dim light, he noticed the door to the capsule moved to close. He rushed to it and stuck his foot in to make it stop.

Blake, his face going white with anger, pointed to the back wall of the airlock. He screamed. "You didn't shut the door into the ship. Never! Never leave that God-damned portal into the ship open. Not even a crack! You stupid sonofabitch."

Arlen turned to see light glowing around the portal to the ship where he'd left it slightly cracked open. With Blake alone in the capsule, and no guards pointing lasers at him, Arlen grabbed the man by his white collar and pulled him face to face into the room. "If you don't return to the transit ship, will they come looking for you on the Benevolence?"

Blake looked like he might faint. "I, uhm, apologize for calling you a... You see... I can't have any contact with the, uh, uh, inside of the ship, and if it's even...."

Arlen twisted the collar tighter and let Blake have a few seconds to think about the situation. He let go of the man and handed him the box. "This is what's left of Thaler. I expect you to show respect."

Blake backed away, holding the box. He passed into the capsule. "Uhm, sure. No problem." He reached behind him, and the door of the Benevolence slid into place.

Muffled sounds came from the capsule as it disconnected. Arlen let out a long breath. He picked up the black notebook and thumbed the pages. He was alone. Well, except for 5,000 freaks.

THREE

The chemically sterilized portal room didn't suit him. Beyond the wall, a ship the size of a city waited for its newest member. The ship named Benevolence housed mutants with unimaginable problems. Arlen tucked the notebook under his arm and felt for the bar that led him to his new home.

He walked around on the metallic sidewalk. A separation, like a street, divided the fronts of the buildings. Did vehicles move along the streets?

Something like a storefront caught his attention. A glass window displayed men's clothes. Did they make their own? Did the Humane Welfare Department provide garments? He tried to picture Samantha's clothes. Her hideous facial feature had surprised him, diverted his observation. He stepped into the store.

The woman behind the counter had a lovely face, soft hair, large eyes. She smiled perfect lips. "Hello."

"I'm new." Couldn't he do better than that for an introduction?

She laughed. "That orange jumpsuit says it all. You must be the new Liaison Officer. Poor Mr. Thaler." Then she sighed. "And now, poor you." She came around from the counter, moving crab-like on turned-out legs, sporting several feet each. "You thought I was almost normal, didn't you? It's all right. It'll take a while to get used to us. I'm Beth. For what it's worth, welcome to Benevolence. It's what we call our...city."

Arlen swallowed hard and extended his hand. "Thanks." He told her his name and a few descriptions of his journey.

"So, Mr. Rowell, I guess you'd like some better clothes. We've had five L O's since I've been here, and that's the first thing they do — buy clothes."

He scratched his head. "Buy...see, that's

kind of a problem."

"You have a credit provided by our beloved Humane Welfare. We all have credits and jobs. Just pretend it's Earth." Her voice became sarcastic. "Happy and healthy, living a good life at the behest of Earth's benign government. And now you get to enjoy it, too. How nice."

"Five Liaison Officers?"

Beth nodded. "I don't know how many served before I got here. I was in the last round-up of survivors—well, the ones they thought worth saving."

"What do you mean?"

"I had recuperated. The mutations don't go away, but we were cured of the disease. The bureaucrats came to the camps checking on the ones who were free of the virus, and the ones still recovering were removed."

"Removed?"

"People on Earth don't know that, do they?" She spoke her words from clenched teeth. "The officials were tired of waiting. The ten Freak Ships were ready to go, so the cured ones were transported, and the sick ones, those who would have gotten better, were removed, like my sister. Killed, Mr. Rowell. The luck of timing." Beth scurried behind the counter.

"I'm sorry," Arlen said.

"Well, it's old history and nothing we can do about it." Beth swept her hand gracefully toward the shelved walls. "May I interest you in a new shirt and trousers?"

Unsettled, Arlen turned to the shelves filled with shirts. He didn't understand the numbering system. His measurements were 16 neck, and 24 arm, 34 waist.

"You will want the other shelf, Mr. Rowell. Those shirts fit three-armed men."

Three arms? He wanted to get out of that store. Total immersion, he told himself. Sink or swim. He glanced over to Beth. "Is it catching?"

"Not now. The virus has died. We could live on Earth without hurting anyone, but we're too ugly."

Arlen pulled a white shirt from the shelf. The label said, "Double arms, regular neck, average sleeves."

"That should fit you, Mr. Rowell. Good

choice. Now over there," she pointed, "are the trousers for men that have normal lower trunks. Mostly in black, some dark blue. The waists are marked in inches. We can hem the bottoms. Please try them on. There's a fitting room behind the curtain."

Arlen parted the curtains. He let out a staccato breath at his image in the long mirror. He closed his eyes and summoned his yoga breathing. Anna Liza, the woman he had loved, would always love, had taught him that. He opened his eyes and looked to the dull metal ceiling. She died from the plague. Perhaps it was better. She hadn't known about the trial or cried like his mother when the jury foreman read "guilty" to the courtroom. What would his beautiful Anna Liza have thought about the hideous orange jumpsuit?

He put the memories of his lost love out of his thoughts, zipped the suit down in one buzzy motion, and stepped from its prison fiber embrace. How long had he worn those underdrawers? Should he ask Beth if the store provided briefs? Boxers? He laughed at his image. A tumble of dark uncombed hair, a two-day beard, and skuzzy grayish shorts. A high school dropout, convicted murderer, and disappointment to his father, here he was, Liaison Officer of the City of Benevolence.

Shaking his head like a dog shakes off water, he let go of his cynicism. The shirt fit, and so did the pants. He left the orange suit where it fell and headed for the counter.

"Gee, a bit of a clean-up, and you'll look handsome, Mr. Rowell." Beth smiled. "That will be a hundred and two B. Dollars." She laughed. "That's what we Bennies called them. Benny Dollars."

"How do I pay?"

"The Benny Bank generates funds like paychecks. We have actual paper dollars now." She stood up a little straighter, showing pride. "Not from Humane Welfare. From our printing press."

Arlen cocked his head. "You've printed your own money?"

"Not to worry. It won't get out of hand. One of the Bennies is a former World Treasury Exec, and he's in charge. You should speak to him." She looked away for a moment. "He's kind of hard to look at, though. Maybe you should wait a while."

Arlen headed for the door. "Thanks, Beth. I should be going."

"Do you know where your office is?"

"Yep. I'm on my way." He stopped and turned. "You have a nice day."

"Thank you. I hope you can have a nice day. All of the L O's before you committed suicide."

"Uhm, thanks," he said and hurried out the door.

He hadn't thought to ask the time of day, but the streets had more people milling about. A pushcart with a sign, Sandwiches, stopped nearby. Instantly people came out of their buildings and formed a line. As he walked toward the three-story building, he paid closer attention to the structures. Small shops, diners, and offices advertised their services. Some of the stores had been painted; others remained the dull metal provided by Earth's government.

Arlen tried not to stare at the worst mutations. They didn't seem to mind. Some of the residents appeared normal; however, bulges, ripples, and strained seams proclaimed the hideousness shielded by fabric. Only a few people paid attention to him. A clock on a post struck a gong sound. One o'clock in Benevolence? He picked up speed. He needed to read that notebook as soon as he got to his, what? Office? He let out a sickly laugh. Golly-gee, a real office. In his Earth store, he'd fashioned a nook behind the bread shelf where his computer and a beat-up, cluttered desk had been the closest thing to an office. Now he had a big one. And an assistant. One with no lips.

FOUR

Samantha waited for him in his office. "Wow, you look better. At first, Mr. Thaler wore a suit. There's a good tailor across the street."

Arlen rubbed his nose. "Okay, there's a tailor, and a Treasury guru, too."

"Mr. Rowell," Samantha crossed her arms over her chest. "The Fall-Out virus was an equal opportunity life-swindler. We have doctors, lawyers, engineers, and religious leaders. We have a large synagogue and several Catholic churches. Small Christian centers pop up all the time. Our city is rather like any city on Earth, except we're repulsive. The government has pretty much left us to do our own thing. They threw us together without a plan or guidance. We've worked it out by ourselves. A mayor and councilmen keep us organized. On the far side of the city, our farms and hydroponic labs reach as far as the ship wall. Every so often, we receive goods, things we can't make ourselves, but other than that, Benevolence is self-sufficient. We cherish our life, such as it is. Earth can't boast our low crime rate or our efficiency regarding recycling." She closed her eyes and drew in a deep breath, followed by a short exhale. "Our suicide rate was high at first." Her eyebrows pinched together. "What would you expect? Taken away from our families with no contact?" She relaxed. "Most of us have adjusted now."

Arlen wished he had an appropriate comment.

"Do you want me to be your assistant?"

"Yes," he said without a beat. "Please."

"Thank you. I have some work to do, papers for you to sign. I see you have your notebook. You'll want to read it. Actually, I'd like to read it after you're done. I could use a good laugh. We'll go over that piece of shit later, and I'll give you the truth."

Again, Arlen wished he had an appropriate comment. "Okay," was all he could manage.

He sat behind his surprisingly nice wooden desk and opened the notebook. Although he had only been in Benevolence for a few hours, plainly, the book lied from cover to cover. Why? If they wanted him to do a job, shouldn't he have proper information? The piece of shit had most likely been written by and distributed to officials who had been forced to deal with the plague victims.

He got the impression Bennies didn't mind being called ugly, repulsive, hideous, or...freaks.

He put down the book and glanced at his desktop. A black leather-like inset gave it a professional appearance. A small screen and the keyboard were centered on the black part. Pressing the screen produced a list of names. He selected Samantha. Her face appeared, and she said, "Yes, Mr. Rowell? How may I help you?"

Wow. "Can you come in here at your convenience to discuss the, uhm, shit, book?"

Shielding her mouth with her hand, she laughed. "Certainly. I'll be there shortly."

Gee, him...with an assistant. Unfortunately

deformed, but he liked her. Perhaps he could get accustomed to...Oh, God, so many! How many? His back rested against the padded chair. The book said each ship housed an average of 5,000 souls. Mutated and deformed. No mention of death tolls. And at least five of his predecessors had died by their own hands.

Samantha knocked and poked her head in, the lipless face of the woman who would help him.

He steeled himself, looked her dead on and smiled. "Let's talk."

They went over the book page by page. Samantha used her hand to cover her mouth when she laughed. Arlen hoped he didn't appear as grateful for her habit as he truly was.

Some of the data had merit. Yes, she said, there were slightly over 5,000. Excluding the suicides, a small number of the residents had died by natural causes and a few accidents. No babies. The Humane Welfare Office somehow had kept them from reproducing. Otherwise, their numbers would have increased because, in the City of Benevolence, the mutants found partners and screwed their brains out.

Since the H W kept their distance, they most likely didn't know how the Bennies had made changes to the "city." Former construction specialists regularly tore out walls from single apartments and fashioned larger, more comfortable dwellings shared by lovers. Furniture makers took apart the wooden pieces supplied by H W and designed clever, smart furnishings.

"How do the big systems work?" Arlen asked.

"I can only answer in generic form. The water and sewage systems clean and regulate themselves. Except for an occasional light bulb replacement, the electric circuitry works perfectly through hydrogen power, which is somehow linked to the oxygen and carbon dioxide production. It's some kind of circular system, changing and recombining. We've never had a problem with our gravitation. All I know is that everything works."

Samantha continued. Bennies bartered services or used handwritten I.O.U.s at first. One of the few things the first Liaison Officer did was get H W to issue credits for employment. Bennies preferred to work rather than receive handouts. When Mr. Rogette, from the World Treasury, arrived, he went right to work starting a financial institution. After a decade, the H W stopped issuing credits. By then, the Bennies had formed their own economy. Samantha didn't believe H W knew about their financial system because H W didn't give a damn. She amused Arlen with her colorful language.

She described how the ships had been in service for twenty years, including the line-up of previous Liaison Officers. Life in Benevolence had been hard on the Liaisons. Arlen gulped at their average shelf-life.

Samantha glanced at the clock on the wall. She explained there were almost no watches because the plague victims had given up their jewelry when they went to the "healing camps."

Arlen asked about the camps.

"It's five o'clock, Mr. Rowell. We don't have overtime here. I'll tell you more another day. I'll leave you with one description. The camps had a crematorium for the non-survivors."

On her way out, Samantha stopped at Arlen's desk. "Tomorrow is Saturday. We don't work on the weekends. Here's your address." She wrote on a notepad. "Mr. Thaler was older, shorter, and fatter than you are. I doubt you'll want his clothes. They can be remade to fit you. His possessions remain in the apartment. Perhaps you should take the weekend and see what you can use. Good luck." She pulled the slender top drawer from his desk to remove two electronic key cards, gently placing them in his hand. "This one to lock the office and this one for your apartment. Good afternoon, Mr. Rowell."

Arlen wished he'd asked her how to find the place.

Out in the street, the number of people had quadrupled, as had the variety of deformities. Fall-out from the bombs had culminated in a worldwide plague. He couldn't ignore the results of war as he was currently surrounded by the proof. Nuclear warheads coupled with dirty bombs riddled with diseases released horrific viruses that thrived on the atomic energies, mutating into hideous disorders. Eventually, the diseases joined forces, producing the Fall-Out Plague, making human DNA go wild, a malady science could not cure. Third-World countries, where poverty and illness had been commonplace, didn't feel the full fury of the infection. Global leaders, however — America, Europe, and parts of China — knuckled under the plague's power. As soon as a person fell ill, he or she rode the ambulance to the camps and were rarely seen afterwards.

He'd attended hundreds of funerals. Those with caskets were displayed inside a plastic Hazmat bubble. For the few open coffin services, viewers kept their distance. Grief wormed its way into Arlen's memory. Anna-Liza. So beautiful, so young. He had started to date her when she caught sick. He fell in love with her on the first date. He had choked up seeing the light auburn hair through the coffin bubble across the room.

Arlen, like the average citizen, thought most of the plague victims had perished. But, ten Freak Ships housing an average of five thousand survivors meant a lot more people lived. Fifty thousand mutated souls sent to the Freak Ships existed in floating metal cities. How did that compare to death?

Arlen, saddened by his thoughts, walked slowly, trying not to look directly at the folks who bustled by. A purring engine noise made him turn around. A small car! No sleek model, this thing was made from put-together parts, wheels, and seats. But there it was, front and rear seats occupied. A quick glance revealed one of the passengers had no feet. Arlen watched the vehicle hum by. His sadness lifted. That car represented the human spirit. Whoever put that car together had risen above the handicaps and not acknowledged barriers.

When he turned back, a man stood next to him. Arlen couldn't help his smile. Perhaps the man didn't appreciate his appearance, but children the world over would laugh at the red ball nose and the white patches surrounding the man's eyes. The overlong shoes suggested matching feet. His white-patched frown iced the cake.

The man shrugged. "Yeah, yeah, I look like a circus clown. Whatever. You hide your mutations well."

Arlen searched for words that wouldn't

materialize. He settled on, "I'm the new Liaison Officer." Before the clown-man could respond, Arlen showed him the address. "Do you know where this is?"

"I'm headed that way."

The man clumped his large feet in an odd stride. Arlen altered his own steps to keep pace.

The man's head bobbed with his steps. "Thaler. Uh huh. Offed himself. Most Normals can't handle it here. We've adjusted. Why can't you guys? You, who have no mutations to deal with."

Arlen halted. "Maybe it's the way we get here."

"What does that mean?"

"Well," Arlen chose his words carefully. "We don't get much time to decide whether we want to come, and then, if I'm an average example, they treat us like dogs, pushing us into the situation with no training or expectations of what we are supposed to do."

"Kind of like getting better from your disease and then being rounded up, cattle-car style, and hauled off to an unknown destination?"

"Kind of," Arlen said. "My family thinks I'm dead."

"Ditto," the man said. "Getting the picture?"

"Very loud, very clear."

Clown man started walking again. Arlen stayed at his side.

"So, who are ya?"

"Arlen Rowell." He thought it best to leave out the convicted killer part. Did it matter that he was innocent? Probably not.

Clown man stuck out his unblemished hand. "Doctor John Watson."

"Doctor Watson?"

"What a bitch, right? Pediatrics. Go figure. My own kids are grown by now with families of their own. I hope."

"What do you do now?"

"Since there aren't any children in Benevolence, I take care of adults. Check-ups, sniffles, infections, the occasional broken bone. Whatever. My clinic is near your address. I'm going there now. The clinic stays open until ten tonight. Sometimes things get rowdy on Friday nights. After dark."

"Dark?"

"Twenty-four-hour light and dark cycle. From the kind hearts of the Humane Welfare. We have a few technicians who have made changes in the temperature and daylight duration so we can have seasons."

"Impressive, uhm, Doctor Watson."

"Yeah, yeah, you've read Sherlock Holmes. Go ahead; let it out. Say it just once. You know, the game is afoot, Watson."

Arlen hoped he'd made a friend because he enjoyed his walk with the clown-man. "Where's your clinic? In case I need medical attention."

"Over there." Watson jerked his thumb to a gaily-painted shop. Its canvas awning had a picture of a clown, a reasonable likeness of the good doctor, and the caption "Doctors-R- Us."

Watson shrugged again. "Why not? Life is short." He bobbed his head. "Laugh or cry. It's everyone's choice. By the way, your building is one street over." He broke away and crossed the street to his clinic. He waved.

Laugh or cry. At that moment, Arlen could have done both. He continued on until large numerals, 1386, painted black on the metallic brown building, said he was home. Apartments A, B, C, and D, occupied the ground floor. He waved the card over the apartment B's entryway, waiting for the click of the lock. The door slid open. Soft lights illuminated the first room. The lights softly lit up in the two other rooms as he checked them out. The apartment had been painted a cool gray. Sparsely furnished, it fully met his taste. Thaler had been a neatnik. No dust. Wait, would a ship the size of a city have dust? Yes, he decided. The small kitchen had a round window over the sink. And a plant! Drooping and brown, but still alive. Wondering how long Thaler had been dead, he watered the thing.

The clean sink had old-fashioned levers, hot and cold. Arlen washed his hands. He peeked into the refrigerator. Wow! Beer. A paper label touting the great taste of Benny Beer showed a three-armed man with bottles in each hand. The label did not cover the chips and scratches of a recycled container. Carefully, he unscrewed the top, hearing the muted pop of carbonation. Just a sip. Not bad. How many months since he'd had alcohol? A while. The Benny Beer tasted pretty good. It would definitely do.

Arlen and his new friend, the brewski, moved to the couch. He stretched his legs, perfect in every way, onto the coffee table. For the first time in, how long? He relaxed.

FIVE

No holovision, no disc players, not even an old-fashioned radio. Humane Welfare? Time for a closer inspection of his pad.

Thaler had left the place ready for a new tenant. Arlen pulled back the simple bedspread. Clean sheets. Ten steps up from the prison mattress. The products in the small bathroom had Benny labels—antiperspirant, aftershave, and a small bottle of dentifrice. Arlen hoped he wouldn't have to recycle Thaler's wooden toothbrush. Where would he get a new one? His admiration for the self-sufficient people of Benevolence grew. If 5,000 Normals came together in a city, could they have accomplished what the Bennies had done?

In the cupboard, dishes and cooking utensils occupied one side, glass jars of food in another. No cans. On Earth, processed food came in plastic trays, heated in seconds. He wondered what Humane Welfare had given the "victims" to eat initially. Space food, most likely. Desiccated powdery yuck stuff. The cheaper rocket lines used it in real-time flights giving unlimited material to stand-up comics.

Arlen recalled the black notebook's description regarding the state-of-the-art systems, requiring no maintenance. The book boasted about the refined air, the clean water, recycled daily to 100% purity. Samantha's description backed up the book's claims, at least the technical parts. Oh, how lucky those survivors were that H. W. looked after them.

Water. Arlen licked his lips. That beer represented his first liquid intake since...the bottle of water in the rocket. He rushed to the fridge and grabbed another Benny Beer. Taking stock of the refrigerator's content, he concluded Thaler ate well. Lettuce, albeit browned, tomatoes, celery, dried-edged greens, tofu. No meat. Would bacon ever roll over his tongue in the ecstasy only bacon can deliver? He wondered how the Bennies overcame that deficiency. So much to learn.

Alcohol on Benevolence had the same effect as Earth — a pleasant buzz. Arlen perused the shelves in the sitting room. Real books! When the war started, the EMP had wiped out computerized stored literature. Books became an expensive commodity. He checked the titles. No classics. He thumbed through a thin book. Benny Press? Shaking his head with a smile, he read the first page. A mystery. Not bad. He continued and read for hours until he yawned. Just a few more chapters. The End. He closed the book.

The small window over the sink had no light coming in. When did it get dark outside? His esteem for the people of Benevolence grew. He showered and rinsed his underwear, hanging them over the rod. The bed summoned him. Sleep came easy.

The glow from the window bathed the kitchen in light when he opened his eyes. He rustled around the kitchen and chuckled at the jar with the label saying "Benny Coffee" and in big letters underneath "NOT." He put a cup of water in the heating unit, spooned in the "NOT" powder and sipped. The label hadn't lied. Not coffee, but it had the same kick as caffeine. Good enough. A loaf of unsliced bread made a fool of him. The uneven piece he managed to cut tasted delicious.

Just as he finished his simple breakfast, a knock on the metal door startled him. "Hold on." He peeked his head around the door.

"How are you doing?" Samantha said.

"Good. Uhm, I need to get dressed. Count to ten and come in, okay?"

She put her hand to her mouth, muffling her musical laugh. "One, Two…"

Arlen scampered into the bathroom. The drawers could have been drier, but he wiggled into them and pulled on his new trousers.

When he returned to the sitting room, Samantha waited, holding a fabric bag. She took a short breath when she saw him.

He checked his zipper. "What's wrong?"

"Not a damn thing. I'm not accustomed to seeing a perfect person." She stared at his bare chest, her gaze running all over him. "You're so handsome."

He hoped the heat he felt inside did not show up red on his face. "Uh, thanks."

She gave her head a shake as if she'd read directions that said, "Shake well before serving." Bag in hand, she said, "The office has a small budget for miscellaneous things. I didn't know what Mr. Thaler left for you. I'm sorry. I was rude not to offer you more information about food and things."

Arlen took the bag and brought it to the tiny round dining table. "Thanks." He pulled out cookies. "Oh, and apples. Trees?"

"When the first wave of survivors, we call them pioneers, came aboard, silos of nutrient powder fed them. In their unlimited generosity, H W provided vegetable seeds and fields of soil. Every so often, the H W clerk brought a bag or two of fresh fruit. You know the size of those capsules, so you can imagine the amount of fruit. We had lotteries. The winners agreed to save the seeds. As we organized, farmers and arborists took over. Some of the seeds germinated into fruit trees. I doubt H W knows about them."

"No meat?"

"We get by on Tofu and protein powders."

Arlen gently dumped the remaining contents from the bag onto the table. "Great! A toothbrush, comb, and a hairbrush. This?"

Samantha displayed the wood item in her palm. "Benny shaver." She opened a hinged top and removed a folded blade. "Made from recycled metal, and you sharpen it like this." She pulled the blade across the rough material stuck to the lid. "H W gave us knives but no shaving blades." She sniffed her derision. "Knives sharp enough to slit our own throats but no razors for hygiene. Even ugly people want to keep clean and neat."

Arlen took the box and slid the razor back inside. "Of course, they do." He picked up each item, homemade but far from crude. "Thank you. I appreciate your thoughtfulness."

Samantha took a step back. "You're different, Mr. Rowell. I'm glad you're here."

Arlen ran his hand through the dark curly mass on his forehead. "You can call me by my first name."

Her lipless slit showed straight, even teeth.

"Okay. Except at important meetings."

He jerked his head. "Do we have important meetings often?"

She put her hand to her mouth. "No. Never!" Her tinkling laughter subsided. "But maybe we should. Mr. Rowell, uh, Arlen, all of the other Liaisons have come to us depressed and disheartened. They meant well, but their despair ended their will to live. They couldn't help us."

Arlen pulled out the chair for Samantha, and when she sat, he did. "Shit. I'm as bummed as I've ever been. I wasn't going to tell anyone, but I beat an execution to come here."

"All of the Liaisons have tragedy reasons. You…killed someone?"

"An accident blown out of proportion." He swept his hand toward the light of the kitchen window. "The Bennies have nothing to worry about from me."

Samantha nodded her head vigorously. "Absolutely. I sense it; I know it. I think you will adjust, and when you settle, things will get better. For you and for us."

They sat silently for a few minutes. "Arlen,

would you like me to take you to a store? My fiancé owns a little market not too far away."

"Fiancé?"

"Yes. I knew him slightly from our MBA program, but a lot of us got sick. I didn't know he was here until we ran into each other at a May Day festival."

"May Day?"

"As best as we can figure, the pioneers arrived on May First. We treat it like July Fourth. Most of the Bennies are Anglos and understand the Independence Day thing. Anyway, you can get whatever you need at Keel's store on credit, and I'll sort out the paperwork. Mr. Thaler left you a hefty balance in his account. Toward the end, he had no interest in buying or going anywhere." She laughed behind her hand. "Not like there's very far one can go, but there are a few places... We'll save that talk for another time."

"All right," Arlen said. "Do you want to show me that store right now?"

She nodded.

"Let me get my shirt and shoes."

She shook her head and sighed. "Too bad

you can't walk around shirtless. The ladies would love it." Her hand went to her mouth. "Of course, men wouldn't take so kindly to it." I'll put this stuff up for you while you get ready."

Within a few minutes, Arlen had shaved, brushed his hair and teeth. He slid his key card in the pants pocket, and they left. Samantha pointed to the shops as they passed. Some had obvious signs. She described the services of the unmarked stores, a Laundromat, a take-out, secretarial services, hair stylists, doctor, dentist, shoemaker, clothing store.

Keel's Grocery Emporium had a colorful striped awning held up by slanted posts. Hinged, the posts could be lowered at closing time, giving the wide entryway a covering.

Samantha commented while Arlen examined the setup. "We don't have much theft, so it's easy to open and close this shop." She took his hand and guided him into the store.

"Hey!" A fellow with reddish nodules on his neck and cheeks hurried to Samantha and kissed her nose. "So, Sam, who's this?"

"My boss, the new Liaison Officer. Arlen

Rowell, may I present my true love, Max Keel."

Arlen extended his hand. Max shook with a hardy, sincere touch. "Ain't she something?"

"She is. Lucky man, Max."

A serious eye exchange between Samantha and Max gave Arlen a tingle. Samantha raised her eyebrows; Max nodded.

"Welcome to my store, Arlen. What can I get for you?"

"I'm not sure. What do you recommend?"

"I don't know about Earth food anymore, but we try to replicate, in taste and texture, what we can remember." Stacked in a glass cooler case, oblong and round loaves of varying shades stood in front of soldier-like bottles. "Here, you have meatloaf, ham loaf, chicken loaf, etcetera."

"Meat?"

"Naw. Dressed-up protein powder. But you'll love the fresh bread. There's a bakery not far from here, and I'm their first stop."

Arlen smiled at Samantha. "The cookies?"

Max took a box from under the counter. "I know Sammy brought you some, but these peanut butter ones just came." Max handed a cookie to

Samantha and Arlen. He took one for himself.

Arlen concentrated on his, avoiding the sight of Samantha eating. "Not bad," he said. "Actually, pretty good."

"Appreciate the cookies; we don't get them too often. Well," Max said. "I've got another customer. Help him get what he needs, Sam. I'll see you later."

Arlen compared this grocery store to the one he'd owned on Earth. All of the bright colored labels on cans and boxes of the Earth store contrasted with the jars and bottles and cloth-wrapped goods in this one. He envied the fact Max didn't worry about securing the place. After the robbery, Arlen heard his store had been smashed and looted.

Samantha handed Arlen a few fabric bags and began loading them. Jars of fruit, vegetables, and ceramic containers holding dull-colored powder overflowed the bag. She recorded the handwritten prices on a paper. Arlen clanked bottles of Benny-Beer together in a quilted bag.

"Now you know where the store is," she said. "Come here when you need anything. Write

the items down—honor system. Now, I'll help
you carry the stuff back. Oh, and keep the bags to
reuse."

Arlen carried the heavier bags while he
made mental notes of where they walked.

"If you'd like to see us having fun, come to
the lake downtown tomorrow for Sunday Picnic."

"Lake? Picnic?"

"Not a lake like you think but we Bennies
like it. Every Sunday, Picnic in the Park." She
turned her head away to laugh. "Come with us
tomorrow. Max and I will stop by one-ish. Don't
worry about the food; we'll have a basket."

"One-ish. Okay."

"You'll get used to our times. Maybe we
should buy you a clock for your place."

Arlen raised his eyebrows. "A clock without
numerals that says one-ish, two-ish, three-ish?"

Samantha halted and deep-gazed. "You are
different. Things will be better."

He shrugged. "I'm no Jesus, so don't get too
excited."

"We'll see, won't we?"

Another "car" puttered past them.

"Clever. A Benny car?"

Samantha strained her neck to catch a glimpse. "Proper generic term, but it has a name. They all do. Not too many cars. Yet."

They walked the few blocks to his apartment and brought in the purchases.

"I really appreciate this, Samantha."

Although her face always looked grim, her eyes sent a serious message. "Max and I will help you every way we can."

Arlen scratched his head. "Uh, okay. Tomorrow?"

"Right. Have a good day, Arlen."

For the rest of the daylight, he cleared out the things Thaler left that wouldn't be useful, making a neat pile behind the couch. This time he noticed the light streaming from the round kitchen window had dimmed. "Twilight," he said aloud. He rummaged through Thaler's book selection, turned on a lamp and read. After dinner, uneven slices of bread and faux meat spread, he finished his book, drank a beer, and went to sleep.

In the morning, he experimented with the desiccated nutrient powder, courtesy of Humane

Welfare, adding a pinch of the few spices in the cabinet. Tolerating two spoonfuls, he threw the mess in the sink, concentrating on the "NOT" coffee and a better-cut piece of bread.

Having no idea of the time, he cleaned up, read, and waited for Samantha and Max. He read for hours before he heard their knock.

For the first time, Arlen noticed what Samantha wore. Perhaps he had become somewhat adjusted to the appearance of the Bennies. Her well-fitting yellow shorts matched the color of her hair and displayed her shapely legs. The curved neckline of her white shirt gave a hint of cleavage. She must have been stunning as a Normal. Something inside him chided. What does stunning mean? Because she has no lips, does it make her less beautiful?

Max wore a plain gray Tee shirt and black shorts. The bumps that studded his cheek and neck were more pronounced on his calves and ankles. Why didn't Max wear long pants to cover the abnormalities? The thing that chided him about Samantha resurfaced. Max didn't hide his defects because he didn't have to. He was what he was.

Arlen tried to keep his facial features flat because he didn't want these kind and good people to see his mixed emotions—disgust and admiration. Is this what drove the other Liaison Officers to take their lives?

Max carried a large basket. Arlen couldn't remember seeing a prettier basket. The colorful woven slats formed an intricate design, and the lid hinged with the same material. Through the weave, he saw baguettes and little fabric-covered jars. The clanking glass, he hoped, meant Benny Beer.

As they walked, they chit-chatted. Did Arlen sleep well? Was he able to make use of the nutrient powders? What did he think of Benevolence so far? He answered and assured them he found the apartment and foodstuffs acceptable.

He didn't understand how they could act so comfortable. They had been banished. No other word described it, from their family, friends, home, and planet. Picnic in the Park? He couldn't imagine what a metallic city, like a prison for five thousand blemished, forgotten people, could offer in the form of amusement. Then they turned the corner.

Six

From his position, he saw an area somewhat resembling a town square with trees surrounding a large sparkling pool. A fountain of multiple sprays rose to a man's height, crossing streams, feathering as they fell.

He gaped for a moment.

"What do you think?" Max asked.

"Humane Welfare did that?"

Samantha blew a long raspberry. "Really?"

"Yeah, I guess not. Benny ingenuity."

Max clapped him on the back. "Right-O. There were houses in that spot. A group of our architects drew the design, and some of us men tore the houses down. Metalworkers trained a bunch of us, and we built this center park."

"Don't you need welding stuff to work with metal?"

Max nodded. "Sure. But the original shipbuilders had to have equipment, and it cost a bunch to bring it back to Earth, so they left it. We found immense underground storage chambers full of tools and materials. What they thought of as trash became a treasure for us."

Approaching the park, they mingled with the crowds of people carrying fabric bags and baskets of food. Sad, Arlen thought, all adults.

The gushing waters echoed against the metal buildings surrounding the park. Without wind to blow mist, he sensed the moisture. He took a deep breath. Odd, no real smells—not like Earth. Of course, filtered air.

"Arlen!" The voice came from behind him, not from Max or Samantha. "Arlen Rowell!" He knew that voice. Blood drained from his face.

He turned.

Weaving through clusters of people, a bald woman hurried toward him. "Oh, God," she said, panting, "I can't believe it. I didn't know you were here—that you caught the sickness."

He couldn't find his words—or enough oxygen.

Anna Liza grabbed his hands, looked him up and down. No flowing auburn hair waved from her movements. No eyebrows came together as she searched for his defects. No eyelashes blinked. Tears formed. She choked.

They stood in silence, both stifled by words that would not form.

Arlen pulled her close, feeling her tremble. Words finally came, not necessarily the right ones. "I, I, I attended your funeral."

Anna Liza pressed her face into his chest. Her pink scalp deepened to red. She pushed away and wiped her tears with the back of her hand. Her expression changed to anger. "Did you now?" Her lips pressed together. "A rumor went around that Humane Welfare used mannequins with wigs under the Hazmat bubbles. They did it so family and friends could have closure. Isn't that humane of them? So, as you can see, reports of my death have been hugely misrepresented."

She stepped slightly back to get a better look. "You…look…really…good."

He cast his gaze to the metal ground, making his oxygen need greater and adding dizziness to his problems. He riveted his eyes on her. "I didn't get the plague." Did he feel guilty because he didn't catch the horrific disease?

Anna Liza turned to Samantha and Max, a question on her hairless face.

Samantha patted Arlen's arm. "He's our new Liaison Officer."

Arlen's shame prevented him from looking directly at her. "I arrived in an orange jumpsuit."

Silence clothed her thoughts. "I don't care what you did." She put her arms around his neck. "I'm so happy to see you." Then she took quick steps backwards and shut her eyes hard. When she opened them, her browless eyes pleaded. She sighed. "I don't know if you're happy to see me."

He sucked in a large gulp of air and pulled her close. "I've never been good with words, Anna Liza, but, truly, I've never been so happy to see someone in my entire life."

A tall man came around a group of people and made his way to Anna Liza's side. His hands sprouted fat rounded fingers looking like pink sausages. A tell-tale bulge under his shirt said he had other gifts from the plague. "Anna Liza, I turned away, and you were gone."

She paled; red splotches colored her cheeks. "Oh, sorry, Jeff. I, uh…"

Arlen stepped between Jeff and Anna Liza. "I'm Arlen." Extending his hand, he worried about Jeff's hesitation to shake.

Jeff raised his sausage hand but held back. "Anna Liza is my…girlfriend." He amended the statement. "We live together." Clearly, Jeff didn't care for what he saw.

Samantha wrapped her two hands around Jeff's giant mitt in place of Arlen. "I've seen you on the basketball court. You're really good."

"Yeah," Jeff said, his tone cynical. "I'm tall, and I have these wonderful fingers. Works like a charm."

Samantha paid no attention to his sarcasm. "Call me Sam, and this is Arlen Rowell. He's our new Liaison Officer. I'm guessing he knew," she had to think for a moment, "uhm, Anna Liza, on Earth. Old friends."

Max came to Samantha's side. "Oh, and this

is Max, my fiancé."

Jeff folded his sausages in front of his chest. "I shop at your store sometimes."

"Right, and I appreciate it," Max said. "How about joining us for lunch? If you bought your stuff at my store, I know it'll be great."

They laughed. Jeff attempted a smile, but it came out as a sneer.

"We'd love to join you," Anna Liza said. She cast a glance at Arlen.

He understood the message.

Not pleased, Jeff said he'd fetch their picnic basket and join them.

With Jeff gone, Anna Liza said, "Arlen. It's so good to say your name. To look at you." Her shoulders sagged. "Jeff is a great guy." Tears erupted from lashless eyes.

"Anna Liza," Arlen whispered. "You and Jeff…"

Her lips quivered. Quietly, so only he could hear, she whispered, "live together. But I still I love you."

Samantha stepped close and circled her arm around Anna Liza. "It'll work out. Dry it, now.

Don't let Jeff see you cry." She shot a look at Arlen, and he understood her message.

Jeff returned, zig-zagging around groups of people, some of them spreading their quilts, some of them passing out sandwiches, others milling about, deciding where they would settle. He held the quilt tightly, not making a move to lay it down.

Max draped his patched blanket over his strong arm. "One nice thing about the Benevolence Park—no sunburn! Is under this tree here good?"

"Good," Samantha assured him.

Anna Liza glared at Jeff. He unfurled their quilt.

Arlen fought with his mixed emotions. He couldn't bear the thought of Anna Liza being mauled by Jeff's ungodly mitts, and he hated his own prejudice. He reproached himself internally, arguing that he would loathe any man who slept with Anna Liza. The image of them together made his teeth clench. He wasn't the only one with internal dialog. Jeff, pale and downcast, looked like he'd lost everything in his world. And maybe he just had.

Max kept the beers cold by wrapping them

in icy towels. He handed the cold brews around. Arlen chugged his. Jeff held his bottle in the sausage fingers and didn't take a sip.

Arlen wiped his mouth on the back of his hand. "So, do you have a job, Anna Liza?"

"Everyone has a job," Jeff said. "She edits books for Benny Press."

Arlen didn't enjoy Jeff answering, but he could play the game. "And what do you do, Jeff?"

He sat up a little straighter. "I pollinate."

Great. Now he'd have to ask more questions. "Well, obviously, I'm new, so I don't know what that means."

"Using a tiny brush, from eight a.m. to five p.m. I move pollen." His voice turned snide. "Snake in the hole, anthers to stigma, you know, sperm-and-egg time."

Anna Liza patted Jeff's knee. "See? These are the bee's knees."

It took Arlen a moment to process. "Oh. No bees."

Jeff shook his head. "Or butterflies, gnats, wasps, beetles, or thrips. Me and a crew keep busy with rotated crops in the fields and the hydroponic tanks."

Anna Liza smiled at Jeff. "He's a botanist, Ph.D. from Harvard."

Jeff's shoulders drooped. He held up his hands. "Before these."

Arlen pictured Jeff bent over flowering plants, holding a brush with those clumsy fingers. The plague had done more than leave mutations; it had scarred people deeply. It had eclipsed their souls.

Samantha moved over and gave Jeff's forehead a nose kiss. "Thank you for your hard work. You and your crew give us real food. Think of what we'd be eating if you didn't work your magic brush." She picked up his malformed hand and rubbed it against her cheek. "So many heroes." She shot a glance at Arlen. "Right?"

"Heroes. A good word." Arlen felt a wave of anger. "And the people on Earth don't have a clue."

Max folded his arms in front. "Some of the people do."

Arlen pictured that weasel, Blake. Of course, it was impossible to know what the former L Os had reported, but remembering Blake's attitude, the man knew and just didn't care. He turned to Samantha. "What kind of reports do we give the H W clerks?"

Max shook his head. "No business. On Sunday, we relax. Ask Sammy tomorrow when she's at work. How about another beer?"

Arlen accepted the chilled bottle and took a long draw. He scooted backwards to lean against the young tree they had chosen for their site. Taking a breath to fully enjoy the taste of the beer, he noticed a line of people walking toward the pool. They carried instruments. "A band?"

Max nodded. "As close as we can come. One of the Bennies had been a stringed instrument restorer. He made the violins, cellos, and mandolins. Someone else made the drums. A music professor rewrote sheet music from memory."

Arlen scratched his head. "Didn't the Liaison Officers ask for instruments?"

Samantha narrowed her eyes. "Of course. Humane Welfare gives us what they think we need."

"How do I get in touch with them?"

Max leaned close to Arlen. "Tomorrow, when she's at work."

"Max," Samantha said, "When I want you to speak for me, I'll let you know. That's a legitimate question."

"Sorry," Max said.

"Arlen, the answer is, we don't contact them. Our only communication occurs when the clerk arrives in his capsule. Sometimes a supply ship comes, but we never see them. We only know they've been here when the silos are full, or things show up in the outer storage clusters."

"They dock?" Arlen tried to picture a supply ship docking with the Benevolence.

"Same set-up as with the clerk. Airlocks. But since we never know when they're coming, we don't have communications with them. I suppose we could leave notes, but actual communication falls to the Liaison Officer—but only during the scheduled visits, meaning twice a year."

Anna Liza took a swig from her bottle. "We at Benny Press, apply for paper and ink. Once in a while, it shows up. Workers from H W won't get near us. They load our supplies on a conveyor belt accessed from the outside skin, probably heavily disinfected lest air from Benevolence gets to them. A conveyor belt brings the stuff into supply areas and gets dumped on the floor of the storage clusters."

Samantha nodded. "All requests for supplies come from the Liaison Office. We fill out forms; the L O presents the requests to the clerk."

"Blake?" Arlen asked.

"Mr. Thaler dealt with him during his entire stay." Samantha sighed. "Four years."

"Wait," Arlen said. "How do we know when he's coming?"

"We have a timetable for his six-month visits. Humane Welfare didn't see fit to give us watches. We've made our own clocks. Except for the usual Benny time, we have to be careful regarding capsule visits because if the L O isn't in the docking room and Blake, or whoever has the nasty job, will wait for thirty minutes—he has a watch—and if no one shows, he leaves. Our Timekeeper, a brilliant mathematician, lets the L O know when to go into the chamber and wait."

She sneered. "Like waiting for a king to arrive."

"So, we have to wait six months?"

Samantha shook her head. "No, he had to make an unscheduled visit to pick up Mr. Thaler's remains. I don't know how Blake knew, but I suspect Mr. Thaler got a suicide note to someone. Blake would have asked Humane Welfare to find a replacement in time to prevent two unscheduled stops."

Arlen chuckled. "Yeah, unscheduled. That must be why he acted so pissy."

Jeff looked at his untouched beer. "They think they'll catch the plague from us."

Samantha shrugged. "Blake's always pissy. If he read any of the reports, he'd know we are free of the disease. Cured. The virus died years ago. By the way, the next scheduled visit is in about a month. Doctor Lass, the Timekeeper, will let you know a few days ahead and then again the day before."

The music began. People on their blankets quieted. Soon they heard the strains of familiar Earth songs and a few that had been composed in the City of Benevolence. Arlen enjoyed his time—except for the parts when Jeff showed his affection for Anna Liza. Those hands, the ones that provided fruits and vegetables, touched the woman Arlen had loved on Earth, had never stopped loving. There she sat in arm's reach of him. He drank more beer.

After the music, games began. Some of the metal deck had patches of soil, and on a few of those patches, bits of grassy plants grew. The gamers carefully avoided the scraggly green. A small area of soil held the stake for horseshoes. Max invited Arlen and Jeff to play.

Arlen bent down and scooped up a handful of dirt. "It's weird to see soil on top of metal sheeting."

"Not to us," Jeff said. He let out a breath and changed his tone to a friendlier demeanor. He described how the Bennies created the topsoil. "When anyone cleans, they save the sweepings. Dirt happens. For real. Dust, skin-shedding, wood shavings, ground glass, whatever, blends into organic material that, when treated, can be soil. We recycle everything. Same with our fertilizers. Instead of jettisoning sewage into space, one of our engineers broke into the sewage plant and rigged it to dump into tanks. Gross though it may seem, our crops and flora thrive on our treated waste."

Arlen recalled the passage in the black notebook regarding the state-of-the-art sewage system needing no maintenance. Would Humane Welfare care that their system had been hacked? What would happen if the tinkering resulted in the system's breakdown? As Liaison Officer, should he report the tampering? No. If H W wanted to know, they'd be checking. He cleared his mind. He hadn't been on the job even one day; now wasn't the time to speculate on the extent of his duties. Tomorrow. He smiled internally because he knew he could count on Samantha. Max had been correct. She was something.

Best he could figure, the crowds broke up around five-ish. The small amount of litter from the picnic impressed him. No paper cups, napkins, cellophane, or the usual detritus, had been left. People took away what they brought. What a concept! Even though Earth folks yapped about recycling and not wasting, they couldn't hold a candle to the Bennies. Should he write a report and shove it in Blake's face in a month?

Jeff rose and extended his ugly appendages to Anna Liza. Arlen couldn't watch when Jeff brushed bits of errant vegetation from her form-fitting jeans and firm breasts. Even without hair, she remained gorgeous. Compared to the other women nearby, Anna Liza was a goddess. When Arlen dared to look, she met his gaze, but he wasn't sure of what her eyes were saying.

"Time to go," Jeff said.

Anna Liza nodded. She smiled and thanked them for the invitation to spend Picnic in the Park in their company. As she folded the blanket, she threw another look Arlen's way. He was sure the look said, "Contact me."

SEVEN

Arlen lagged a few steps behind Samantha and Max on the way back to his apartment. He'd only been in Benevolence a few days, but so much had happened. It left him forever changed. He grimaced. He could have been forever dead.

When they reached the apartment, he invited his companions in. Sam and Max rifled through the pile of discards left from Thaler's occupation. Max shoved a few items into his basket.

Sam pulled aside a few pieces of clothing. "You can have these altered."

He felt strange asking his assistant about underwear; however, his need for information outweighed his timidity. "Where can I buy some briefs?"

The question didn't bother Sam at all. "I'll make some calls for you." She held up a pair of cotton shorts. "You may have to wear some of Mr. Thaler's boxers until you get your own."

She put her hand to her mouth and giggled. "It's not like anyone will see you in them."

Arlen instantly thought of Anna Liza. Would she ever see him undressed? He shuddered at the memory flash of Jeff's lumpy shirt. He looked at the thin carpet of the living room floor, ashamed for that thought.

"Well," Max said, bringing Arlen out of his self-imposed disgrace. "We're headed to my place. See ya,"

Max's place? They didn't live together. Sam had called Max her fiancé, but Jeff had referred to Anna Liza as his girlfriend. They weren't engaged! But they did live together. Life on Benevolence was as complicated as Earth, albeit with different complications.

After they left, Arlen rinsed his clothes while he showered. Dings from a warning bell indicated the water would stop in sixty seconds. Ironically, the only timepiece in the place monitored his allotment of water. He wrung the garments and flapped them over the rod. Keeping the towel around his waist, he searched for reading material. Nothing invited his attention. Anna Liza interrupted all of his thoughts, including the worry he would not get up at the right time in the morning. He wished Anna Liza would come to his bed. Among fulfilling other needs, she would know when to awaken.

Arlen had no trouble getting up the next morning. Like all apartment buildings, he had neighbors. Metal walls didn't exactly dampen the racket. The vents pulsing shared air brought smells of toast, heated oils, and "NOT" coffee.

He experimented on a breakfast, tidied, and walked to work, joining the many others who seemed happy to be on their way to their places of employment.

Someone had unlocked the office. When he entered his room, he found a single flower, a white roadside weed-daisy he'd seen growing on Earth. It sat in a chipped-rim ex Benny-beer bottle with a simple fabric bow. A card nearby said. "Welcome, Mr. Rowell. The staff." Arlen felt a lump in his throat. A flower. That meant a lot here. He wondered if that species was self-pollinating, and then he pictured long, fat fingers, not with a fine brush, but wound around Anna Liza. "Don't do this," he muttered.

He pressed the screen to summon Samantha.

"Good morning," she said, entering. "I see you made it here without an alarm clock."

He chuckled. "I had an alarm clock…of a sort." Pulling his finger lightly over one petal, he looked up at her. "I appreciate the flower."

She leaned closer. "It's all perspective, isn't it? What's a nuisance one place becomes a prize somewhere else."

They shared a quiet moment. "So," Samantha said, "do you have plans for today? What would you like me to do?"

"I should meet the staff."

"Perfect answer, Arlen. Let me get them."

After a few moments, she returned with three people. "Arlen Rowell, please meet Ray Dothan. He keeps track of the requests, meaning he helps people fill applications for requests to Humane Welfare." She rolled her eyes, "not that he has a lot of success in getting what they want."

Arlen shook hands with Ray. The furry hair on the man's arms rippled. Bald patches here and there on his neck and chin showed pale, thin skin underneath.

Samantha patted a woman with curly brown hair. "Meet Candy Piscatelli. She catalogs all medical reports, marriages, and deaths. Also, she keeps track of our citizen's addresses, employment, age, etc."

"Nice to meet you, Candy," Arlen said, trying not to look at the partial third eye winking on the woman's forehead. Why did she wear her hair pulled back into a ponytail? It would have been so easy to conceal the thing.

"And, this is Oscar." Samantha guided the older man forward. He used a metal cane and lumbered on huge legs more suited to a hippopotamus. "He's our accountant. Not that this office has a lot of financial responsibilities, but Humane Welfare initially gave us stipends, and now we earn salaries. Oscar keeps track and deducts taxes."

Oscar leaned on his cane and held his hand

out toward Arlen.

Arlen pictured the clothing shop. Perhaps Oscar shopped in the wide-leg aisle. "Glad to meet you, except for the tax part, Oscar."

Oscar spread his free hand. "Death and taxes. Don't worry, it's minimal, the taxes, I mean. So far, we don't need a police force or fire brigade. Our taxes predominantly cover city improvement." Oscar's face became solemn. "We think it is important to make life worth living, and we're willing to pay for it."

Arlen glanced around. All of his staff had the same sober expression. "I agree completely. We should make our city as agreeable as possible."

She didn't smile, but Samantha's eyes softened with approval. "Oscar will give you a report on Mr. Thaler's account, which you will inherit." She cocked her head. "Strange, isn't it? You inherit the sum total of a man's work you never knew existed. But, "she clapped her hands together. "Benevolence can be strange, especially if you're new. Okay, everyone, chop, chop, let's get to work."

Ray, Candy, and Oscar left. Samantha pulled

a side chair close to Arlen's desk. Clearly, she had something on her mind.

"Arlen, when you commented about the taxes, you referred to Benevolence as 'our' city. Did you mean that?"

"I'm here. I'm a Benny now."

Samantha looked to the ceiling. "Praise God, or whoever sent you." Moving her eyes from the ceiling to him, she stared for a moment. "I know this is sudden, and I'm taking a big chance, but we don't have a lot of time. It's less than a month until the capsule comes."

Arlen braced. Somehow, he wasn't surprised. He didn't know what they were planning, but he would learn shortly. A revolt. He'd sensed it the minute he met Max. "What's up?"

"Max can give you the details, but we want to hijack the capsule and take over the transit ship."

"What? You have a militia trained to go to war with the transit soldiers?"

"No militia. In fact, not one of us Bennies has been in the military. We don't think that's an accident."

"Do you have weapons?"

"Crude, but effective. We're depending on the element of surprise. We take Blake—no problem—pull out everything possible in the capsule and cram it with our men."

"Why the transit? We can't possibly go back to Earth."

"Who says we want to go to Earth? There are other planets. The transits can go interstellar and find a place. Plus, the transits have computers with information. If we can get the ship's plans, Benevolence can bring us there. We want a real home. If not an uninhabited planet, one where humanoids won't think we are so strange looking."

"Wow. A new planet. Dream big, I always say."

"That's part of it. We also need to find out why we're sterile. It doesn't do any good to live in paradise if we die of old age with no one to follow. The answer might be in the transit computers."

Arlen ran fingers through his hair. "What do we have to lose?"

Samantha slapped the desktop with both hands. "Our lives, including yours if you go along with us. Most likely, H W wouldn't tell anyone what we tried; they would just ignore us completely. No visits, no supplies. After all, I'm close to thirty. In seventy years, most of us will be gone. Some of our people think that's the plan anyway. We don't reproduce, and eventually, we go away. The empty ships would stay dormant until new undesirables need them."

He pondered for a few moments. What about Anna Liza? He wanted to marry her, raise a family. What did he care where? A new planet would be fine. They could pioneer together. What if the plan failed? If he was killed? Then he would have died trying to make a better world for her. A jolt of anger pulsed. She'd still have Jeff, Mr. Harvard.

Being part of the rebellion would provide status, something better than high education. He didn't need to think about it further. "I'm in."

Samantha dropped her head and took a breath. "I knew when I first met you, Arlen." She returned the chair to its place. "I'll bring you the reports from the past Liaison Officers. You should read them to understand our history. Don't discuss what I said with anyone I don't approve of, okay? Work as normal. Some Bennies won't like this idea. Fortunately, you are the only one who could rat us out." She paused, looking him over. "But you won't. I know it."

"Look, if I'd stayed on Earth, I'd most likely be dead. They don't have death row prisons anymore. Straight from the courtroom sentencing to the death clinic. I'm no fan of the government or the Department of Humane Welfare."

She didn't comment but left quietly and shut his door.

Arlen gazed around the room. Not for the view, but for something to do while he let the hurricane in his brain die down. The clock on the wall made a soft hum. Did Max and his revolutionaries know what they were doing? The thought of Anna Liza interrupted his maelstrom in the form of another brain hurricane. If he helped the Bennies, he'd be helping her, the woman he'd loved on Earth and continued to love in the good ship Benevolence. She deserved a real home, and if it wasn't with him, then Jeff.

Did the revolutionaries have a chance? What

kind of weapons? Crude, but effective? Guns? Look what a gun did for him. A smile crept over his lips. Even if nothing else came of it, he'd love to see Blake's face at the takeover. Poor guy would probably shit his pants. The capsule, though, was very small. How many could cram in? He didn't know much about piloting space ships, but all Blake did was flip a few switches. The automatic drive did the work.

Samantha pushed in a cart filled with files. "This ought to take you a while. These are the reports prepared by our office for the H W clerk. The files hold the lists of supply requests. See this skinny file? This is a record of all the requests fulfilled." She butted the cart up to his desk. "Concentrate on this material, and try not to think about Operation Freedom." She shrugged. "Corny, I know. Truth can sound foolish."

Arlen picked up a file and flipped it open. He had questions, but they didn't come together in a reasonable form. "I…uh."

Samantha patted his arm. "Max will see you and explain the details. Put it out of your mind for now."

"Hmm. Out of your mind? Good phrase."

"Don't think we haven't used that multiple times."

They shared a quiet moment before Samantha left. He tried to focus on the report in his hand. Interjected thoughts of Anna Liza fought with the mental picture of armed men jammed into a space capsule. His stomach did a flip. "At least I'm not dead," he muttered. "And, I've found Anna Liza."

He forced his attention on the reports. The afternoon flew by, interrupted only by a break for the food cart outside the office. Tacos filled with vegetable protein did not taste like beef and bean. Food had become fairly unimportant in the big picture. Along with the taco, he tried Benny Cola. Not terrible. He downed the last swig and returned to the reports. At the end of the day, he smiled at the stack of files he'd read. He hadn't thought of himself as the executive type, but here he sat behind a desk in his own office with an assistant and staff. Yes, he would probably be killed in the attempted coup to be perpetrated—neat word, he thought—but when it went down, aside from his brief romp with the punk robber, he would be standing up to something. He wasn't quite clear, however, on what that something was. Oh, yes, freedom. Okay, freedom works. Especially if it helps Anna Liza. Would it?

EIGHT

Each day Arlen learned more about his job as Liaison Officer. Although he wished to hear the details of Operation Freedom, Max hadn't met with him. Even when he shopped at Keel's Grocery store, Max didn't say anything. Arlen didn't ask questions. It had been two weeks since Samantha told him about the plan, but it wouldn't do to push.

He focused on the work. Once he'd read the reports compiled by the previous Liaison Officers, he began his review of request applications. Sewing machines, glass jars, art supplies, a bottle-capping appliance, all reasonable petitions. He'd find out how many had been satisfied in the skinny file.

One morning, as he flipped through the tall stack of applications, a name caught his attention. Anna Liza Ross. She had requested paper and ink. He had her address. Yeah, maybe Jeff's address, too. He wished he knew Jeff's last name. He summoned Candy.

He squirmed a bit at this new situation being boss. As soon as Candy passed through the door, Arlen asked, "Do we have a list of employment, uh, I mean, how many engineers, nurses, botanists, etc.? Addresses?"

Candy didn't flinch. "Of course. I'll get it right now."

What would he do, show up at their door? He had to see her. Had to. He needed to know more about Jeff.

Did he believe in coincidences? Minutes after Candy brought in the long list citing citizens and corresponding data, Samantha buzzed, saying he had a visitor. Anna Liza had come to him. She showed up with a basket of cloth-wrapped sandwiches and Benny colas.

She pulled something else from her basket. "Hi. I brought you lunch and the latest publications from Benny Press. Two mysteries and an adventure." She handed him the slim volumes. "We have a couple of romances if you want them."

A quick wave of his hand meant he would not be reading romances. He checked the cover of the top book. The artwork showed spacemen battling over the surface of a rugged planet. A large ship, shiny and bean-like, hovered in the distance. The idea distracted him for a moment. Did Max and his rebels have company? How many folks living in Benevolence dreamed of their own planet?

"Arlen?"

"Sorry." He thumped the novel. "I look forward to reading it."

He unscrewed the cap to the cola and held it toward her.

"Oh," she said. "Right." They tapped bottles in a somber toast.

Arlen's mind tossed silent words around, trying to get them right. Struggling with what to say, the idea of food lost its appeal. He put down the cola. "Anna Liza," he began.

Anna Liza stared at her bottle and made a

face. She placed hers on the desktop. "I can't stand it, Arlen. I've been miserable since that Sunday."

"Crap," he said.

"I don't know what to do."

"Has Jeff proposed?"

The question made her flinch. "Not exactly. It's more or less assumed. We've lived together for three years. He's a good man. I know he loves me."

Arlen thudded his elbows on the desk. "And you?"

She looked down at her hands. The wait killed him. An invisible belt held him to the chair, preventing him from grabbing her, professing his devotion. He wished he could talk, show her his softer side. Maybe he should read those romances — use them as tutorials.

She searched him with her eyes.

Words flew from him. "Anna Liza, I love you. Have since the moment we met and didn't stop at your funeral."

Her eyes grew large, adoring. Tears formed, splashed on her cheeks. She pulled a napkin from the basket and wept.

The invisible belt thwarted him. He should caress her, offer comfort. Suddenly she shot up from her seat and ran out of the office.

"Shit," he said loudly. He wanted to stop her. She hadn't declared her love. Did she belong to Jeff? With his stomach flip-flopping, he drummed his fingers on the list of occupations. Where his fingers rat-ta-tatted, he saw the page of botanists. He pulled the list closer and studied it. Geoffrey Pendleton, Botanist, Ph.D., Harvard. Reading the man's stats didn't help Arlen's mood. Jeff could have run for president with his merits. Among other accomplishments, he had achieved the rank of Eagle Scout. Arlen folded the list and let it hit the desktop. "Shit," he said.

He let out a long breath. That would be the end of researching Doctor Pendleton. How could anyone compete with those creds? Not him. Plus, as a newly recruited rebel, he might not be around for that long. He couldn't involve Anna Liza in any way. Pushing the files to one side, his glimpse of the space adventure cover confirmed his feelings. Spacemen at war.

He tried the sandwich. Was no taste worse

than bad taste? He'd skip lunch. Maybe dinner would be better.

At five o'clock, Ray, Candy, and Oscar said good-night.

Samantha leaned against his doorframe. "Max wants to see you."

"Here?"

"Why not? He'll arrive in a few minutes." She maintained her position, her eyes riveted on him.

When someone stared, his first impulse made him check his fly. "What's wrong?"

"Nothing. Do you believe that all things happen for the eventual good?"

He scooted his chair back on their small wheels. "Hell no. Was the plague fair? How about my conviction? You don't know the details, but...."

"I don't have to. I know you didn't kill anyone on purpose."

"Really?" He drilled his stare into her eyes. "But it would be okay for me to kill transit soldiers on purpose?"

She straightened her stance. "Who said

anything about you going to the transit ship?"

He pulled back a few inches in his seat. "I thought Max was recruiting me to join the… rebellion."

"Well, he'll tell you what he wants." She leaned away toward the office entryway. "He's here now."

Max approached and slid his hand around her waist. "Hey, baby." He kissed her.

Arlen watched the loving exchange. He wanted that, too. He recalled the nights he spent in Anna Liza's embrace, nuzzling in the sweet smell of her luxurious hair. Jeff hadn't experienced that. His nanosecond of superiority crumbled at the realization that Jeff lived with her now.

Max took the seat recently vacated by Anna Liza. He waited until Samantha left and closed the door to speak. "You still in?"

Arlen nodded. "Talk to me."

"In a week, that asshole Blake will dock the capsule outside the entry room. As soon as the ship's door seals, you immobilize Blake and signal us to come. We'll have tools to strip the shuttle. Then as many as can will cram in and head back to the transit ship. You force Blake out of the entry room into Benevolence." Max smiled unpleasantly. "He'll love it here, won't he?"

"What happens when you get to the transit ship?"

"Not sure. We can only guess at what the transit is like, but we think it's only lightly defended. They won't be expecting us. Surprise is our only advantage."

"Suppose you can get five men in the capsule, and all five get out into the transit. What then?"

"Thaler said he didn't see more than twelve soldiers on the transit. We take a few hostages, and we'll kill whoever gets in our way to find the main computer. We have some experts here in Benevolence who can retrieve information. You've been here, Arlen, what, maybe three weeks? Have you noticed? No computers? They, Humane Welfare, don't want us to have access. No radios, no means of communicating to anyone on Earth, or ways of researching a single thing. While our computer man finds what we need, our armed men...."

"Our rebels?"

Max shook his head vigorously. "Our rebels will find the ship's control station."

"Then what? Don't you think Earth will retaliate? They may send military ships."

"Thaler said those transits have plasma weapons. We'll have hostages. Let Humane Welfare try to attack." Max winked and smiled. "We'll be waiting. Truth is, though, they probably don't care that much. They lied to families when they said a lot of us were dead. They can't very well say a ship full of living freaks had enough balls to hijack a transit vessel. Think, Arlen, how much did you ever hear about the Freak Ships? Humane Welfare can't afford to have us in the limelight. People would start asking questions. News shows would start investigating. No, I doubt H W would do a thing. They'd cut their losses and clam up."

Although hijacking a transit craft represented lunacy, Max made some sense about what H W would likely do. Nothing.

"Max, they'd stop filling the silos with protein powders."

"True. We'd have to find a planet before

too long. One that would support our crops and hopefully have game."

"Wait. How would you get there? I don't understand."

"The man who was Liaison before Thaler had a relative who helped design the Freak Ships' drives. Our ship has FTL capability, or we wouldn't be here, where ever in space we are located. We need a computer to get the data to pinpoint our location and engage the FTL. Then we can go anywhere."

"I don't understand. Why would the builders leave the FTL in a Freak Ship?"

"It's there, but not working. That Liaison's relative feared exactly what has happened — human beings stranded in space without control over their own lives. An underground railroad, you might say, cared about us and left us information for our escape. You haven't seen what exists beneath our feet."

Arlen had wondered about that. "Tell me."

"When you first got here, you noticed that the roof of our great city-ship is painted blue like the sky, right? The ground," he tapped the floor with his foot, "and what lies on top represents two-thirds of the ship. The rest, one-third, lies below. The ship's power center and all of its workings are under us. We've explored most of it and found booklets and instructions hidden all over. That's how we changed the sewage system. Those underground railroaders concealed help for us. And they knew someday we would be ready to use what they left. First, we must get to computers. The transits have them."

Arlen didn't know what to say.

Max engaged his eyes. "So, will you seize Blake for us?"

"I will. Tell me what to do."

"Get a big knife."

NINE

Between his frustration over Anna Liza and the impending coup of the transit vessel, Arlen didn't have a waking moment's peace. The mayor's summons didn't help his anxiety.

Arlen walked to the town hall, a two-story building painted white. An imposing clock tower, with real numerals, not ishes on the face, made the building more distinguished. The floor, painted in faux marble, impressed him. A mural on the wall behind the receptionist's desk showed a rendering of Sunday in the Park, crowded with folks enjoying the fountain.

The receptionist, an attractive dark-haired woman, showed no signs of mutation. "The mayor's ten o'clock appointment? Ah, yes, Mr.

Rowell. You may go in." She pushed back her rolling chair to point the way.

What Arlen could see of her shriveled legs, withered feet brushing the fancy floor as she moved, gave him a start. "Thanks," he checked the name sign, "Miss Hopkins."

She stiffened. "Mrs. Hopkins."

"Oh, uh, okay. I'll just go now."

He knocked at the door. A muffled voice bid him to enter.

The mayor did not stand when Arlen entered. His eye gesture indicated no invitation for Arlen to take a seat in the three chairs adjacent to the wide, elegant desk.

"I'm Maurice Lewis, Mayor of Benevolence."

Arlen extended his hand to shake.

The mayor's pause to respond sent a message stronger than words. With obvious reluctance, the man finally shook hands. "You are our connection to the Earth," Lewis said. "Some of our citizens don't think we need Earth or Humane Welfare."

He didn't care for this man's tone of voice or facial expression. This summons did not represent a "welcome to our fair city" or anything cheery.

Arlen's words came unexpectedly. "So, are you an elected official, or did H. W. give you the office?"

Mayor Lewis's face went bright red.

Self-appointed, Arlen thought, or he wouldn't have reacted like that.

The mayor bit his lip, allowing his color to wane. After a few moments, he said, "I have a gift for you."

Arlen flinched. Had he judged this man wrong? Was this an example of the split-second temper that ruined his relationship with his father?

Mayor Lewis pulled something from the kneehole of his desk. "A briefcase made especially for you." He leaned over, stretching to put the item in Arlen's hands.

Arlen accepted the gift, a bright orange bag well-sewn with handles and an open top. Clearly visible on the side were numerals, his prison identification numbers.

Arlen hadn't misjudged the man. He unclenched his jaw. "Thank you, Mayor. How about that! My suit's been recycled. Great fabric and the color is so bright I won't have any problem locating it." He brushed a spec from the soft case.

"I'll be going now. If I ever have a chance to serve you, make sure to come by my office."

Arlen turned his back on Lewis. On the way out, he bid goodbye to Mrs. Hopkins. He was careful not to emphasize the word "hop," which could have been a joke in poor taste.

Back in his own office, the waiting reports offered him a distraction. Distraction until his eye caught the bright orange of the mayor's gift. He made a mental note to steer clear of the city hall's official.

He let his work keep him occupied until Dr. Lass advised him of the time to meet with Blake. On the appointed day, he waited in the entry room, staring at the green light to signal docking. A device rigged to signal the rebels huddling close to the entrance felt slippery in his hand. He had not experienced sweat since he'd been there. Moisture from stress, not heat.

Having no previous contact with the shuttle, Arlen had no idea how long he should wait. His recollection of the few words Blake said to him made him think Humane Welfare, or perhaps Blake himself, came when they wanted, as long as the date worked. He wished he'd asked someone if the transit and shuttle clocks coincided with Benevolence time. He chuckled lightly. Would they call it "Benny Time?"

He had developed a fondness for all things Benny. The cola, beer, the...

The light flashed green. Arlen wiped his sweaty palms on his pants and gripped the device. He tensed at the metallic screeches. The capsule was docking. Standing, he took a quick breath. A metal-on-metal slide meant the shuttle's door had opened and the door in the skin of the ship Benevolence cracked, on its way to admitting Blake.

One hand held the device, the other, now behind his back, clenched a knife. The weapon, well-honed by a Benny shoemaker named Ralph, one of the four rebels who waited on the other side of the entry door with Max. As soon as Arlen captured Blake, the rebels would gut the capsule and return in it to the transit ship.

The door fully opened, with Blake filling the entrance. But someone else was with him. Someone clad in a hazmat suit. In a blur, a white-cloaked arm pushed Blake out, and he skittered across the floor. Arlen squeezed the button, but before Max and the men could clear the chamber's opening, the doors between the two conjoined vessels had shut. Clanking and groaning, the ships separated.

Blake lay on the floor, barely moving. Max, stern and impassive, rushed into the chamber. His eyes pressed Arlen's for answers.

Arlen shrugged.

Ralph drew his weapon, something like a machete, its edge gleaming even in the soft light of the entry chamber. He kneeled next to Blake, putting the blade close to the man's face. After a moment, Ralph turned Blake on his back.

They took a collective breath. Blake's face dripped with pus-filled carbuncles. He moaned.

Max's head movements to the men had them take Blake by the arms and drag him through the portal into Benevolence City. "The clown doctor is the closest clinic," Max said.

It happened so fast. What had happened? If he wanted answers, he needed to leave and follow Max. Arlen rushed through the opening into the daylight and blue sky of Benevolence City. He remembered the location of "Doctors R-Us" and hurried to catch up with the rebels who had not had their chance at rebellion.

The town appeared normal. Lunch carts served clients, a few folks tread the sidewalks, and only the small group ahead of him who carried Blake seemed out of order. By the time he caught up, they had disappeared under the colorful awning into the office of Doctor John Watson.

The four rebels sat in the waiting room. "Max is in there," Ralph said. "The doctor told us to stay. We can't go anywhere until he knows what's wrong with the clerk."

"Blake," Arlen said.

"Right." Ralph cast a glance at the closed examining room door. "Blake."

A woman in a white uniform wearing a name tag, "June Dispinetti, R.N.," came from the office. "Our guest doesn't look so good. Fever off the charts." The ridges of extra skin on her face wrinkled with her words. The same pleated flesh covered her hands and the part of her arms exposed under her sleeves. Brown eyes with long lashes revealed the last vestiges of extraordinary beauty. "Wash your hands, fellows. We must assume he's contagious. We'll all be quarantined for a while." Her shoulders sagged. "Sorry about that. No problem for me. It's not like I have a husband and kiddies at home."

Nurse June didn't have a husband. Benevolence practiced the custom of marriage like Earth. Did dressmakers fashion lovely lace dresses for weddings? Arlen doubted it. The Bennies tried to keep social customs, but they were practical. What would one do with a gown after the wedding? Make tea towels?

Nurse June offered Benny-tea or coffee NOT, and all four men accepted. Arlen took tea, something much closer to the Earth beverage. He hadn't been in space long enough to forget Earth's foods and tastes. He wondered if getting used to the NOT would be a good thing or if losing the memory of real coffee's taste was worse.

Arlen sipped his second cup of tea when Doctor Watson came out of the room. He addressed the quarantined occupants. "I have Blake stabilized. He's in a bad way, and I don't know if he'll pull through. Mr. Rowell, he's asking for you. Go on in."

"Me?"

Doctor Watson nodded and sat down in his own waiting room. June brought him a cup of NOT.

He quietly pushed open the door where Blake lay on a gurney. The running sores on the man's face made Arlen's stomach turn. Blake raised his hand, beckoning.

Arlen swallowed hard. "You wanted to see me?"

"You bastard," Blake croaked. "I got the plague because you left the door cracked. You have me on your conscience if you have one. I probably gave it to others on Earth. Because of you." Blake turned his head and vomited. Blood mixed with bile trickled from his mouth.

"Doctor Watson," Arlen called.

Watson and June came into the room.

Arlen hung his head. "I left the door ajar when he brought me here. He's caught our plague."

"No way," Doctor Watson said, his clown mouth turning down. "This isn't what we Bennies had. We never had sores like that. This is a different plague."

"You're sure it wasn't because the door to the city let in the air?"

"Absolutely. Wasn't it nice that Humane Welfare sent him here? What are we supposed to do with him? The researchers on Earth have a better chance at coming up with a medicine for this...whatever it is...Blake's Disease, we'll call it, than we do in Benevolence. Our pharmacy capabilities can barely support our needs. We make our own ether and chloroform for simple operations. We grow penicillin, and I've given him that already. We can't do any more than that for this man."

June patted Arlen's arm. "You didn't do anything wrong, Mr. Rowell. Come on, let's leave our patient in peace."

"Yep," Doctor Watson said. "I've given him what opium I had to ease his pain. He'll sleep now."

June's hand still on his arm, Arlen turned to the doctor. "You have opium? Humane Welfare supplies that to Benevolence?"

"Hell, no." Doctor Watson almost spit the words. "Thaler got seeds for opium poppies smuggled to him. I'm sure the clerk who took the bribe to bring in porno mags had no idea seeds had been attached to some of the pages. Ben/Ag grows the poppies, and the pharmacy boys cook it."

"Mr. Thaler did that?"

"Yep. He had a cousin who worked on the transit ship. The cousin could get a message now and then, and he wanted to help. Thaler had money on Earth and could pay for bribes. He cared about us, but eventually, missing his family so much and seeing how we struggled made him depressed. He just couldn't handle it."

"Sorry, Doctor Watson. I can't replace Thaler. I don't know anyone or have any connections."

Doctor Watson locked eyes with him and stared for a moment. "Yep. But, no prob-lem-o. Word is you're one of the good guys."

That made Arlen's head jerk. Was the doctor in on the rebellion? "Uhm, me?"

June smiled at him warmly. It sparkled, way past the creased flesh of her face.

Watson shook his head and sat back down in the waiting room. "Junie, girl, we best make some beds up for our guests. I'll stick the flag up outside to summon the runner."

Arlen returned with Doctor Watson and June into the waiting room. "Runner?" He had no idea what Watson meant.

Max showed him a two-sided box near the doorway. "If we have a quarantine problem, we put up the flag. It sticks out, like old Earth mailboxes. The first person who notices it tells the mayor's office. They send a rescue party to find out the emergency. We'll talk to them through the filter on this box. We don't have phones yet on Benevolence. The Emergency Department in the mayor's office will handle everything for us. Our families and friends will get word. The department will provide meals, fresh clothes, that kind of thing. We all understand the importance of quarantine."

Doctor Watson cast his gaze around the room. His white-rimmed smile turned up. "I still have those girlie magazines, if anyone's interested."

The quarantined rebels looked at each other. No one seemed interested. Did they no longer wish to see perfection? Were they happy and satisfied with their mutated partners? Arlen's esteem for these people jumped two notches.

Max rubbed his neck, disappointment about the hijacking clothing his face. They'd have to wait six months before another capsule came.

June took good care of the occupants of the Doctors R Us clinic. Two days later, Blake died. Arlen helped June unload the refrigerator in the clinic's small kitchen. Watson and Max folded the man's body as best they could and crammed it into the cooler.

"Well, there goes any cold stuff. Oy! No chilled Benny Beer," Doctor Watson said.

June pursed her full lips. "Think we can get a new fridge, John?

"I hope so. I don't care what we use to disinfect it. I won't be able to eat anything from that box now." He distorted his face, which for him gave more impact. "Now, put up the flag again, Junie. We'll send for the Death Squad."

Arlen felt the blood drain from his face.

"Death squad?"

Doctor Watson laughed and really looked clown-like. "Don't get your knickers in a knot, Rowell. It's a Bennyism. We have some morticians who deal with bodies. Interestingly, they rarely get a chance to practice their skills because now that our suicides are waning, we have few deaths. We had to be healthy to meet the Freak Ship qualifications, and the air is pure. We're a clean city, so very few illnesses." Doctor Watson thumbed toward the back room. "Of course, we've got a doozy now, don't we? If I thought Humane Welfare people had a semblance of complex thought, I'd suspect they turned Blake loose to doom us. But Blake had a thing or two to say."

"Really?" Arlen leaned in closer, hoping the good doctor would share.

"Okay," Doctor Watson said, stretching his blue-patched arms wide. "Blake came down with his disease two weeks after bringing you here. The incubation period of the Freak Plague is three days. If he caught something from us, it would have shown up earlier. You were with him in the capsule and had to sit close to him, I imagine. So, if he had it when you came in the capsule, you would have gotten it, too. He caught this thing after he left Benevolence."

Arlen silently chuckled at Watson's term Freak Plague. "You don't think it's Freak Plague?"

"I don't. No one had sores like that. Plus, the Freak Plague took a long time to diminish. It changed DNA during the process. Running sores do not indicate grossly altered DNA. Blake had something different. Maybe there's a new plague starting down on our old home."

"So, we might get it because of Blake?"

"Yep. We should know in a few days if we'll catch it. If any of us gets a fever or has any signs, we all need to stay here until we die or get better. We can't turn it loose in Benevolence." The doctor's face, with the look of a clown, became serious. "We can't let the Bennies suffer another plague. We'll do the right thing."

Arlen's blood had once again begun to drain from his head. "Right thing?"

"Yep." Doctor Watson was matter of fact, and he turned his gaze to each of the rebels and June. "If one of us dies of this, we end it here by our own hands. The last one alive sets the office on fire. Even in space, extreme heat kills pathogens."

No one said a word. No one showed opposition.

The next day, Max and the other rebels had visitors. Doctor Watson's wife came and, like the others, talked through the small filtered box near the door wearing a mask.

No one came to visit June. With the exception of a quick wave from Samantha, Arlen had no callers, either. Maybe Anna Liza didn't know. That's how he rationalized it. But he had been on Benevolence long enough to know news, both good and bad, spread fast by word or through the newspaper. He wondered if the sickness made headlines on the tri-weekly newspaper, the Benny Herald.

Three days later, Doctor Watson gave the all clear. The Death Squad, masked and clothed in protective overalls, came for Blake's body. Max and his rebels went home to their loved ones. Arlen returned to his apartment. Alone. The Bennies had found partners. Not all of them, though. Nurse June had no visitors during the quarantine. Caring and attentive, she deserved love. Did her solitude in Benevolence match his?

TEN

Doctor Watson had released them on Saturday. The next day would be Sunday, Picnic in the Park. Arlen considered packing a lunch and going to the town center. He hadn't been there since the time Samantha and Max invited him. The day he saw Anna Liza...and Mr. Eagle Scout, Doctor Pendleton, the Pollinator. Arlen buzzed aloud like a bee in disrespect to the Harvard man. Who was he kidding? Jeff was Captain Wonderful. In spite of the funky fingers.

What would be the point of staying in the apartment? He'd already read Thaler's entire book collection. The local bookstore would be closed on Sundays like most of the other businesses. No holovision or canned music. If he wanted amusement, he'd have to go out. Other than intimate pastimes, plays, concerts, and public gatherings entertained the Bennies. Shouldn't he have entertainment, too?

He rifled through his cabinets, packed a lunch, and wrapped a few beers in the wet cloths the residents kept in their fridges for the purpose. Clever, those Bennies.

On his way out, he met the neighbors. He had not become so accustomed to the mutations that he didn't stare, at least for a moment. Folks stared at him, too. Those who didn't know who he was searched him with their eyes. He was different. A perfect man in a mutated world.

As he walked, thoughts of Anna Liza insinuated their way into his mind. She no longer had her beautiful auburn hair. A small price to pay for life. Besides, her beauty wasn't marred by the loss of hair. She was as close to perfect as anyone he had seen on Benevolence.

Each time he thought of her, his loneliness increased. He wanted to do something for her, demonstrate his love, like join the rebellion. If he had caught what Blake had, he would have taken his own life to protect hers. Such a rebellion. Instead of an uprising, they found quarantine. The rebels would have to cool their heels for another six months, that is if Humane Welfare came at all. If they blamed Blake's disease on the tiny opening of the ship's door, they might not continue the deliveries of protein powder and whatever else they bestowed upon the Bennies.

He turned the corner. The view of the fountain, its watery noises and misting edges, softened his turmoil. Bennie pairs lounged on blankets in outward radiating circles, the closest to the fountain being the thickest population. A band, the members carrying their instruments, wound in serpentine fashion through the sprawl of humanity toward the small stage.

He scanned, looking for Anna Liza, flogging himself because of the search. He should leave her be. She had wisely chosen Jeff, intelligent, a man working for the betterment of Benny-Land, and worthy of Anna Liza's affections.

With his mind nowhere other than skimming the crowd for a woman he should not be lusting after, he didn't notice the tugging on his pant leg.

Aiming his gaze downward, he saw June sitting alone on a multi-colored quilt.

"Oh, uhm, hi, Nurse Dispinetti."

She rolled her eyes. "Call me June."

"Oh. Uhm. All right. Nice day, eh?"

She chuckled. "Every day is perfect, Arlen. We live in Mutant Paradise."

"Right," he said, wishing to pull at his collar. Not that it bothered him, but to help dispel his tension. He stiffened, wanting to leave, but her eyes pleading, 'Please don't go' froze him to the spot. As his brain ran a diagnostic on what to do, a couple, far enough away for him not to completely recognize, caught his attention. They ambled closer. Of course, Anna Liza and Mr. Wonderful. Great. Why did he feel a sudden despair? Hadn't he just a minute ago looked for them?

He smiled weakly at June. "May I join you? For a while, anyway?"

She hopped on her butt cheeks, moving over a few inches. "All day would be nice."

He sat and put his fabric lunch bag next to hers. "Help yourself to anything."

"Thanks." June rifled through the bag. "Beer.

Great." She removed the chilly cloth and handed the first one to Arlen. "What else?" Unfolding small towels, she uncovered a sandwich and sniffed it. "Peanut butter. You must make a good salary."

He hadn't thought about the costs of food. His apartment and grocery allowance came from Humane Welfare. Plus, Mr. Thaler had left a sizable bank account. The peanut butter had already been in Thaler's pantry. Arlen hadn't looked at prices on anything. Not the new clothes he'd ordered or the ones from the apartment he had altered. All purchases had been "Put on the account."

"There's two." He said. "Have them both."

"I'll have one. I doubt my meatloaf lettuce wrap will be a fair trade." She passed him a stuffed rolled green leaf.

He bit. "Not bad." He took another bite. "Meatloaf?"

She laughed. "In name only. You haven't been here long enough to forget Earth food. Usually, the taste goes from yuk to tolerable, to not bad, and then after a few years, good. I'm waiting for delicious."

He appreciated her humor. For the few minutes they discussed food, he had forgotten Anna Liza and Wonder Boy. He ate half the roll. "It's really not bad, and I've only been here a few weeks."

"Must be my secret ingredient."

"Really? You have a secret ingredient?"

"All cooks do. But for a sweet talker like you, I'll share. I used NOT in the protein powder, along with beef flavoring."

He looked at the brown stuffing inside the leaf. "I haven't been able to get out of yuk stage for the NOT to replace coffee. How long does that take?"

June leaned back on her arms and let her head fall back a bit. "I couldn't tell you because I hate it, too. If only we could get coffee beans. I know the arborists could grow them. Of course, buying real coffee would most likely end up exorbitantly priced like peanuts. They've only had the peanuts for a few years and use what most they have as new growth."

Arlen cast his glance to where Anna Liza and Superman sat. I wonder if Pendleton gives her peanuts instead of jewelry. Then he smiled.

"What's funny?" June asked.

"I pictured a man standing outside a woman's apartment door on Valentine's Day with a huge heart-shaped box full of peanuts."

June pulled her knees up and wrapped her hands around them. "What an idea. It would work. You're brilliant."

Never in his twenty-eight years had anyone called him brilliant. He took a long look at June. The pleated skin didn't hide her loveliness.

"You're staring at me."

"I know. Does it bother you?"

"Only if my mutation offends you."

"What mutation?" Arlen said.

"You really are brilliant." June took a big bite from the peanut butter and apple jelly sandwich. "And you're rich. My mother would say you were a catch."

"Really?"

She laughed quietly. "Even if you are perfect."

The band began to play something he recognized. Classical maybe. Wadding a towel for a pillow, he lay on the quilt. He wiped a bit of sweat from his brow. Music had always soothed him. He must have heard this piece in elementary school because it brought back memories of that time in his life. Losing himself in a pleasant recall, he summoned a picnic day with Anna Liza, where he remembered brushing back a wisp of her luxurious hair an errant breeze ruffled across her forehead. His mind rushed back to the present. No breeze. No hair. An uneasy feeling made him rise and look over his shoulder.

Anna Liza had spotted them. She stared at June, who sat upright watching the band. Arlen went up on his knees, and Anna Liza moved her eyes to him. He swallowed hard. Using one of the Bennie cooler cloths, he wiped more sweat from his face.

June held a bottle. "Beer?"

He took it, but it didn't cool him down. He couldn't take his eyes off Anna Liza.

Jeff slid his arm around Anna Liza's shoulders. She turned her attention to the band.

Arlen's stomach cramped. His head began to spin. He put the half-full bottle on the blanket and lay back on the quilt with his head on the pillow. He closed his eyes.

"Arlen?"

He barely heard June's voice as blackness closed his periphery. "Arlen! Help me, someone. Please! He's passing out."

ELEVEN

Arlen had vague recollections, mostly blurred lights and muffled words. He became aware that the muted moans he heard came from him. He opened his eyes.

June bent over him. "Hi, there, sleepyhead." She touched his forehead with a small device. "Great, no more fever. You're recovering."

He found his words. "Recovering from what?"

Dr. Watson came to the bedside. "Blake's Disease. For a while there, we didn't know if you'd make it."

Arlen's first thought was Anna Liza. Would she get it? He hadn't gotten close to her. He tried to sit, but he'd never felt so weak before.

June took one side, and Dr. Watson took the other and sat him up. The bed back moved up as June stepped on the pedal. They gently released him against the upright mattress.

Dr. Watson took his pulse. "Nice and steady. Good."

Arlen's thoughts became more organized. He spied the large, nasty sore on the back of his right hand. "Blake's disease?" The memory of the quarantine brought back the part when they talked of sacrifice. He hung his head. "I should do the right thing, Doctor. But why didn't you let me die? You know...for the good of Benevolence."

Dr. Watson's face usually looked humorous, even more so when he pursed his lips. "Let you die? It goes against an oath I took. I also follow the ten commandments." He smiled wide, a U-shape slit against the same shaped white area. "Mostly."

"So, it's up to me," Arlen said as he let out a long breath.

"I guess," Dr. Watson said, his smile increasing. "Nurse, bring a sharp knife."

June smacked Watson's shoulder. "Stop it, John." She shook her head. "You're better now.

No sacrificing."

Arlen looked around the clinic. No other beds had patients. "I'm the only one?"

"So, it seems," the doctor answered. "I let you guys out of quarantine too fast. But luckily, no one else has it." He handed Arlen a newspaper. Front page had Arlen's photo, his title, and a description of his malady. "Everyone knows about Blake's disease, and as you can see, we've asked anyone with a fever or signs of sickness to come to the clinic. No one has come."

Arlen handed the newspaper back to Watson. "At least it's not deadly."

Dr. Watson's clown eyebrows went up. "You know this because...."

"Because I'm still here."

"You're here because I have a crackerjack assistant." Dr. Watson nudged June closer to the bed. "She's an O.R. nurse and more familiar with surgery than I'll ever be. She does most of the surgical treatments in Benevolence. I just supervise. But this time, she shone beyond her skill with the scalpel."

Arlen looked at June. The gathered folds of

skin on her face pinked.

"Yeah, yeah," Dr. Watson said, "take your due, Junie." He patted June on the back. "She deduced if only you contracted the disease, then Blake's is a new form of the plague, and we must be immune. She gave you an infusion of her blood. In my humble opinion, her plague antibodies saved you. I believe Blake's disease is fatal. Fatal to those who don't have Freak's Plague antibodies." He handed Arlen a second newspaper. Front page described Arlen's recuperation.

"I have real work to do," Dr. Watson said. "Call me if you need anything." He left the room.

Arlen put the newspaper to the side. "Thank you for saving my life, June."

"You're welcome," she said as if she'd just handed him a glass of water.

Anna Liza wouldn't get the disease. His shoulders relaxed, and he lay back on the upright pillow. More questions surfaced. "How long have I been here?"

"Two weeks," June said. "Since there's no one at your place to take care of you, stay here until you can return to work."

He glanced around the clinic. Four empty beds pushed against bare drab-colored metal walls. No windows, a few cabinets in the same drab color. No comparison to the cozy apartment, but he wouldn't be alone. "Thanks. I appreciate your kindness."

June folded the newspapers. "You had some visitors."

His mind raced — Anna Liza. She read about him in the news. "Really?"

"Samantha and Max. Nice people. They genuinely care about you."

"Oh." He looked at the sore on his hand. "Nice to know. Anyone else?"

"You mean that bald woman you had cow-eyes for?"

"What?"

"Come on, Arlen. Your stare could have drilled holes in the air. It was written all over your face. You knew her on Earth, didn't you?"

"I wanted to marry her but didn't get around to asking before she contracted the plague. I wept at her funeral."

June's pleated face tightened. "I wonder

how many cried at mine."

"Did you leave a family on Earth?"

"No, I married my career. I regret not having a family."

"We all have regrets."

The morose conversation halted when a bumpy man in gray coveralls rushed into the clinic. "Arlen Rowell? Liaison Officer?" He held a letter. "I have something for you."

Arlen accepted the letter. On the outside decorated with a fancy shield, the emblem of Humane Welfare gave it an undeniable official standing. His name and title had been written by hand. He opened it. The message indicated he had been summoned on the date to appear in the entry chamber, clad in the hazmat suit, which has been provided.

He turned to the messenger. "Where did this come from?"

"The message was attached to the hazmat suit. I found it on the floor in the storage cluster supply room B, along with printer's ink and paper. Sometimes Humane Welfare leaves stuff, probably when they load the protein powder into the silos."

"What day is it today?"

"Wednesday, April 13," June said.

Arlen turned the letter over in his hands. "They want me to be there next week."

"I guess we better work hard at getting you back to snuff," June said.

"Yeah. I wonder what they want." He looked at the messenger in coveralls. "Thanks, man."

"Sure," he answered and left.

"Do you think they want Blake's body?"

"If they do," June smirked, "tough tarts. We don't have his body, just a box of cremains."

Dr. Watson released Arlen two days later. He looked forward to returning to the office so much he came in early. Samantha must have kept tabs to know he'd be back because once again, a roadside daisy waited on his desk. A bow and a note saying, "Welcome back, Boss," made him smile. The smile faded as he thought about being summoned to the airlock room in a few days.

As soon as he heard activity in the cubicles, he pressed the screen. "Samantha, would you come in here?"

Within a minute, she appeared. "How are you feeling?"

"I'm doing okay." He handed her the note from Humane Welfare.

She nodded. "Max will want to talk to you."

"We have another chance to take the transit."

TWELVE

On April 18, Arlen wearing a hazmat suit, waited in the dreary entry chamber. According to Benny-time, it was morning, nine-ish. He brought reading material, but couldn't concentrate, picturing the second attempt to take the transit. His stomach flip-flopped at the unmistakable thud and metallic scraping, meaning something had docked outside.

Arlen pushed the button on his device, signaling Max and company on the Benevolence City side of the chamber to get ready. When both portals had opened, one for each ship, Arlen pushed the button twice. As a hazmat suited person stepped through, Max and his unsuited men rushed in from the opposite side.

"If you're planning to get into the transit ship, I wouldn't," a woman's voice from the speaker in the suit said. "We've got signs of the new plague in there."

Max held his weapon at his side. "So, it'll be easy to take the capsule and get to the transit."

The suited woman shook her head. "No capsule. We've docked this time, the transit ship, H WS. Monitor."

Max lifted his weapon.

Arlen raised his hand. "Wait, Max." He turned to the woman. "Signs of the plague? Hey, I know you. You're the woman in the courtroom who...."

"Loren Drutz."

"What's going on?"

"We have to know what happened to Blake."

"You mean after you shoved him in and slammed the door?"

"We didn't know what else to do. We were afraid he'd give the disease to all of us in the transit."

Arlen had to press his hands against his thighs to keep from grabbing the woman. "But no problem infecting the people of Benevolence?"

"Well, it's not like...well. Never mind that. How many of your...people have survived?

Arlen crossed his arms over his chest. "One."

"All the rest died?"

"Only Blake died. One person, me, the Normal from Earth, contracted the disease, but as you can see, I'm fine."

Loren Drutz's helmet moved slightly. The small light in her headgear showed her face in deep thought. "I see. If no one but you got it, then the Plague Survivors must be immune."

Arlen let the sarcasm in his voice have full rein. "So, it seems."

Drutz stiffened. "A lot of the crew is sick, dying perhaps. Earth won't let us come back."

Arlen stepped closer. "What do you want from us?"

"Help us. How did you combat the disease?"

"We have a way."

A movement in the suit suggested Loren Drutz had stamped her foot. "If you know how to combat the disease, you can save the ones who are sick. Share your knowledge. We have researchers aboard, and they have equipment."

"How do you think we can help you?"

"Why are we wasting valuable time? Let us in for treatment this instant. I'm in charge, so me first. I don't have it yet, but I need to stay healthy."

Max stepped up. "We're taking the ship."

Arlen flushed. "Wait a minute." What kind of power did the Liaison Office have? Life or death type power? He swallowed hard, twice. What did they owe Humane Welfare, the branch of government who sent them into space? The Bennies hadn't been cast out because they carried an infectious disease. The victims had recovered. Humane Welfare banished them because they were deformed, ugly to view, not wanted on Earth. What did Arlen owe Loren Drutz?

The transit ship had soldiers and staff. How many employees of H W were like her? The members of the Monitor crew were men and women, not decision-makers, personnel, and like the mutants, had been stranded in space, abandoned, and sick. He wasn't like Humane Welfare.

Max's face got closer to the helmet. "Arlen?"

"Take the ship, but first, bring the crew inside. Take the soldiers under armed guard. Have one of your men notify Dr. Watson. Tell him we've got...." He turned to Loren Drutz. "How many?"

"Seventy."

"Tell Dr. Watson to have his and all the other clinics ready to receive seventy people. Some have Blake's Disease." He returned his attention to Drutz. "We will evacuate the transit and bring what medical equipment you have aboard into Benevolence."

Arlen could barely believe what had happened. He didn't figure himself as a "take charge" kind of guy. But there he was, delegating responsibilities.

He made the office the command center where Samantha, Candy, Oscar and Ray advised him. Max suggested they get Howard Stadler, a computer expert, into the Monitor to get all of the computers. The newspaper sent a reporter, and Arlen gave her an interview, insisting she include a plea to volunteers for blood transfusions in her story.

Benevolence had five small, staffed clinics, including "Doctors R Us." The medical buildings overflowed with the staff from the transit. The well-stocked sickbay from the transit provided needed equipment and medicines.

After the newspaper hit the streets, citizens of Benevolence lined up to donate their precious antibody-laden blood. Arlen went from clinic to clinic, checking on the progress.

Over the next few weeks, the tide turned for many of the Monitor's crew. A few died, but most of them recovered, and the ones who hadn't contracted the disease had received transfusions as well. They showed no signs of infection.

Once she had received the transfusions, Loren Drutz, Commander of the transit ship, complained about the accommodations, the food, and the boredom of life in Benevolence. Max considered her a prisoner. Arlen considered her a pain in the ass; he confined her to the Monitor.

Some weeks later, after the crew had regained their health, Commander Drutz demanded to meet with Arlen. He sent a guard to escort her to the office.

She marched in, pulled the chair next to his desk, and sat down unsmiling, condescending. "Rowell…"

"Mr. Rowell to you," he countered.

"What? Very well, Mr. Rowell. I have contacted Earth with the news that I have a cure for the disease. They demand I bring the research back."

"Oh, really? You have the cure? That honor goes to Nurse June Dispinetti, not you."

"Whatever. Would you like to return to Earth?"

"Me?"

"You and whoever would like to go back. Amnesty for everyone."

"Amnesty? We aren't criminals."

"Choose another word, then."

"Okay," Arlen said, clenching his teeth, "guinea pigs, ambulating stores of antibodies. I don't think so, Ms. Drutz. No citizen of Benevolence will return to Earth."

"Who are you to make that decision?"

"The spokesperson for the Bennies. And I'll ask you to ambulate back to your accommodations aboard the transit. I don't want you causing trouble in Benevolence, stirring up the people and promising them things you won't deliver. You and your crew need to leave right away, but no one in Benevolence is going with you."

She rose abruptly. "We'll see about that."

THIRTEEN

After the door slammed, Arlen pressed the screen on his desk. "Samantha, I want to speak with you."

Samantha appeared within a Benny minute and pulled the chair still warm from its previous occupant. "What is it?"

"I need to have a meeting with Max and his…."

Samantha put a hand to mouth to laugh. "His rebels. They love that title, you know."

"Good. I'm glad they do because we might require some real rebellion."

She leaned closer. "Why?"

"Because I believe we're in for some trouble."

"I'll go to the store and get him. I'll send out

messengers for the others. I've not seen you this grim before, Arlen."

"I've not felt this way since I got here."

Samantha rushed out of the office. He heard her speak to Ray and Candy, who left with her.

While he waited, he turned over Loren Drutz's words. Earth. The big carrot in front of the unsuspecting donkeys. What could he do about it? No one had actually put him in charge, but he was the Liaison Officer, the mouthpiece for the Bennies. And why would the Bennies want to return to the place that shunned them? Were they any more attractive now? Would they suspect, like he did, that Loren Drutz would keep them captive only to drain them of their precious antibodies? He couldn't and wouldn't take the chance.

In less than an hour, Arlen had his office filled with Max and his men, the Benny Rebels.

Arlen cleared his throat. "I think we're in for some trouble. Now that the crew of the transit ship has overcome Blake's Disease, they'll want to return to Earth." He scanned the room. No one seemed concerned. "They're offering to take Bennies with them."

Questions appeared on the rebel's faces.

"Don't you understand? This is Humane Welfare we're dealing with. They don't want us to return because they've had a change of heart and feel bad about banishing us to the Freak Ships. All they want is our blood."

Some of the rebels nodded their heads. A few murmured agreements.

Max gestured for attention. "Arlen's right. I've already heard rumors that we are heroes and deserve a hero's welcome. Another rumor has it that the government will give us back pay for the years we've been in space. I say that's a bunch of shit."

Ralph, the shoemaker, clapped Max on the back. "I'm afraid a lot of Bennies will believe those lies. We have to do something."

"We'll go to the Town Council and the mayor," another rebel said.

Max shook his head. "The mayor can't wait to board the ship. He wants to be first."

"Then we need to become the law," Arlen said. "Like a governmental coup."

"Ooh," Ralph said, "Guerillas!" He laughed.

"And, you, Mr. Liaison, become the Guerilla Leader. A dictator."

"Me?" Arlen shook his head. "I'm no dictator."

"Martial law," Max said. "We have weapons. It's for the Bennies' good."

Arlen took a long hard look at Max. "What kind of weapons?"

"What we made originally. And what we took off the transit ship. Heavy-duty stuff. That ship was armed to the teeth. But now we, the guerilla Bennies, have the weaponry."

Arlen sunk back in his chair. "Max, do we have the computers out of the transit, too?"

Max nodded. "We've had them out since the first day. Howard Stadler made a thorough sweep of the ship."

"Good. Now what we need to do is round up the Normals, send them back to the H WS. Monitor, and off they go, back to Earth."

Max cocked his head. "Send them back? Shouldn't we keep the transit ship? That's what we planned originally."

"We wanted to take the ship to get to the

computers. Now that we have them and the weapons, we can do without the ship. And we definitely need to get rid of the Normals. That Drutz woman has already stirred trouble."

Max shook his head. "Yeah, but there'll be a whole bunch of Bennies who aren't going to like that."

Arlen sat tall in his chair. "Then round up all the Bennies who side with them." He let out a long breath. "Jesus, that may include the mayor and town council people. So be it. Any of our folk who protest about not going with them to Earth, take them to the park and keep them there. We'll need armed guards." He closed his eyes and dropped his head, mulling over his words. He stood and crossed his arms in front. "Has to be. No Benny leaves. We're not their test rats, which is what I'm certain they want us for."

The room stayed quiet for a while. Arlen pointed. "Max, you are General of the Armed Forces. Anyone have a problem with that?"

The murmur in the room had a positive sound.

Arlen winced. "I don't know much about

military, so you, the initial group, work it out. If you can, recruit trusted allies, those folks who understand what Earth really offers." He pursed his lips and said as solemnly as he could muster, "Dis-missed."

General Maxwell Keel marched his small army out of Arlen's office.

Samantha stood at the doorway, her eyebrows raised in question. "Arlen?"

"Get an umbrella, Sam. A large amount of shit is about to hit a rapidly rotating fan."

Fourteen

Arlen sat at his desk, not sure of his next step. He took a legal pad from his drawer and made notes. He didn't know all of the names of the rebels. He chuckled to himself. Did George Washington, when he was commander-in-chief, know all of the soldiers? Could he compare himself and the Bennies with the fledgling country trying to break free from tyranny? Or was he, Arlen Rowell, the tyrant? He made more notes, partially to occupy his brain from slipping into lunacy but also to keep his plans ordered.

Samantha knocked. She peeked her head inside the room. "You have a visitor, sir."

Mayor Maurice Lewis stomped in. The stomping came from the partial second left foot he gained from the Freak Plague, but there was no mistaking the look on his face. "What in God's name do you think you're doing?"

"Mayor Lewis," Arlen began. Should he play it soft and reasonable or slam it out? He recalled their first meeting. Slam, he decided. "Do you think Earth people want Bennies back to assuage their guilt? Hell, no. They want your blood. They will confine you and drain as much as they can, just short of death."

"What are you talking about? Ms. Drutz has promised us back compensation, living quarters, and formal apologies for our dispossession. Most importantly, they'll fix our mutations."

Arlen sneered. "Dispossessed? Is that the word for what they did? And, Mayor, they aren't going to fix mutations."

"How do you know that?" Lewis said.

"Look, if you can't see it right in front of you, I'll make it easy. I'm enacting a new law. No Benny leaves."

Lewis banged his hand on the desk. "You have no right to make laws. You can't decide for us."

"Well, I have decided. So, either go back to City Hall and keep your mouth shut or join the people at the park, under guard."

"Under guard? With what? Butter knives? We have no weapons."

"Yeah…about that, Mr. Mayor…" Arlen pulled at his lip. "We have them. Among other things, plasma rifles."

Lewis stiffened. "But, will you use them?"

Good question. What would happen if a rebel discharged a plasma gun in the town of Benevolence? Not a real town, a metallic chamber, a bean-shaped ship the size of a city surrounded by fields.

Rosettes of nodules on Lewis's face turned purple. "Well?"

"Don't force our hand, Mayor."

Lewis turned and stomped out, his partial left foot making dragging sounds between the stomps.

Samantha stood as the mayor passed. She flinched when he banged the door behind him. "Not good, Boss."

Arlen sighed. "He is e Pluribus Unum as my

father would say, meaning one of many. I can't believe I'm quoting my old man."

"We all use the tools our parents gave us. Before this happened," she traced her finger around the place where lips had once been, "I had started to see my mother in the mirror. My mother...died from the plague."

"Sorry about that, Sam."

"You've got enough things to worry about, so don't waste energy on me."

"Yeah. I have some pretty pissed-off Bennies and more to come. By the way, I've had Drutz confined to her quarters. When did she have the opportunity to tempt the Bennies?"

"Confined, but able to have visitors. She sent for the mayor and whoever else she wanted."

A noise at the front door grabbed their attention. The frosted glass panel showed a blurry form. The door cracked open, and a shiny pate reflected the lights from the ceiling.

"Arlen?"

Anna Liza! He sprang from his chair and hurried to the outer office. "Come in."

She nodded to Samantha. "May I talk with

Arlen in private?"

"Certainly," Samantha said. "I'll be here at my desk, Mr. Rowell."

"Uh, yeah, thanks." He escorted Anna Liza into his room. "Here, Anna Liza. Sit." He pulled out the visitor's chair, one that had seen much action that day.

Closing the door quietly, he turned to her. "How are you?"

A long trail of moisture ran down both eyes. "Oh, Arlen. Please! Please. I must go back to Earth."

His shoulders sagged. "Oh, that." He shut his eyes hard, summoning words to explain.

"Arlen! Listen."

He opened his eyes and engaged hers, those beautiful large turquoise gems now dripped with tears.

"You don't understand what it means to us, to me."

He gritted his teeth. "You're wrong. I understand perfectly."

"Loren Drutz…"

Arlen dreaded that name.

"She has talked with me."

"She sent for you?"

"Yes. And I really need to go back with her. You see, she said my mutation, my hair loss, would show the people of Earth that we aren't that awful. In fact, once I get hair transplants, I will look completely normal. I can be the spokesperson for all of the Bennies, and the other ships, too. I'll be famous. And Humane Welfare will sponsor all the medical procedures. I'll be pretty again. Not just me, but everyone."

"Anna Liza, think about what you're saying. First of all, you are beautiful, just as gorgeous as you were before the plague. So are the rest of the Bennies, and the people on the other ships, too. Beauty isn't in hair, or someone's skin, or, arms, or anything like that."

"You're not listening, Arlen. I will have my hair back. Don't you understand how important that is?"

He shook his head vigorously. "I understand Loren Drutz found your weakness and used it against you. She lied, Anna Liza. How can you have hair transplants when you don't have any hair."

Tears ceased, but Anna Liza shot daggers from her expression. "Details. Just small inconsequential bits. Loren promised. You will let me go with her. You will. I'll find a way to get around your...stupid...edict, law, or whatever you call it, your illegal restriction."

He squatted close and took her hand. "I'm protecting you. Please believe me. It's for your own good." He swept his arm toward the office. "For everyone's good. Anna Liza, I would never do anything to hurt you or keep you from happiness. It's just that—"

She shot up from the chair. "Liar. If you really loved me like you claim, you would let me go. In fact, you would go with me." She softened her tone and replaced her hand in his. "We can get married. We'll be together. A perfect man and a perfect woman. An important woman who represents all the plague survivors."

His heart skipped a beat. "You'd leave Jeff behind and marry me?"

"Of course. I love you. I want to be with you." Her face hardened. She barely moved her lips. "Not here. Earth. Where we belong."

Turmoil swirled in his brain. The love of his life begged him to be with her. The thing he wanted most in the...universe... within arm's reach. All he had to do was...

"No. You can't go. We wouldn't live in a nice house with lots of money. You wouldn't represent anyone except lab rats. We'd be locked in experimental rooms, drained daily. You're not going. Not you, not me, not anyone."

She pulled her hand out of his grasp and flew through the door. She made the same slam as the mayor before her.

"Shit!" He yelled and sat hard on the chair, making it slide away from the desk. "Shit! Hell! Sonofabitch!"

Samantha ran in. "Arlen. Are you okay?"

He tunneled his fingers through his hair. "No. I'm not okay."

Noises from the outer office meant Candy, Ray, and Oscar quietly headed for the door. Arlen slunk back in his chair, ashamed they heard his outburst.

"Don't worry about them." She leaned close.

"Look. It's quitting time. Go home; get some rest. Tomorrow you'll have to face the crowd in the park and explain why you won't let them leave." She put her hand to her mouth to hide her smile. "It's lonely at the top, Boss."

He rolled his eyes. "Okay. See you tomorrow."

Samantha closed his door. Arlen waited until his heart returned to regular beats. Lonely at the top? When did he get to the top? He grabbed his bright orange briefcase, locked the office, and headed to his apartment. Lost in thought, he barely noticed anything on his way home. He didn't hear the footsteps behind him until too late.

Huge vice-like grips on his neck pulled him into a corridor between buildings—a metal alleyway. His feet dragged and then lifted off the platform the Bennies called ground. The fabric case made a soft plop. His head bounced off the wall, making a metallic echo, but he hit so hard he barely heard the noises.

He saw his attacker. The vice grips on his neck were, in fact, large sausage-shaped fingers, and the handsome face of the six-foot-plus pollinator got so close his breath ricocheted off Arlen's cheek.

"I'm going to kill you," Jeff said.

Arlen tried to swallow. Jeff loosed his hold enough for Arlen to speak. "Why?"

"So Anna Liza and I can go to Earth. Get married."

"Jeff," Arlen, still suspended a few inches, pulled at the man's giant wrists. "Stop."

Jeff dropped his head, releasing Arlen. He slumped. "I can't do it. Even if it means she'll leave me."

It took a second for Arlen to process the experience. Less than an hour before, Anna Liza had begged to marry him and go to Earth. Is that what she told Jeff, too? Was Jeff so in love he would agree to murder?

Arlen jerked his neck side to side and cleared his throat. "Look, Jeff. Think about it. Do you really believe that Drutz woman means what she says? With your intelligence, does it ring true? She wants Benny blood. She is in charge of all sorts of laboratories and medical facilities. She'll get rich selling antibodies as a cure for the new plague."

Jeff averted his eyes and took a step backwards. Silently he slinked away.

Arlen, paying more attention, carefully made his way home.

Fifteen

After a fitful night, Arlen arose and went to work. He stopped at a street vendor and bought a cup of NOT to get the jolt he needed to face the day. The vendor who normally said he'd put the drink on a tab, this time, demanded payment. Arlen had just enough scrip to meet the price. No trouble. He took the NOT, choked it down, returned the cup, and headed to the office, keeping watch of his surroundings. Not a good way to start the day.

When he arrived, people waited for him. Welcomed guests. June, in her crisp white uniform, chatted with Samantha, and Howard Stadler, whom he barely knew, chatted with Oscar.

"Good morning, Boss," Samantha said. "You have visitors."

"I see. Good. Why don't you two, no three," he aimed his words at Samantha, "come into my office. I'll get chairs." He breathed a sigh of relief. These folks were on his side.

Howard, when he turned his head to the left, had a perfect face. Something looking like lichens covered the right side and appeared to grow down his neck. The ear on the lichen side truly resembled cauliflower, bringing to mind the condition old time boxers suffered. Arlen had progressed to quick glances at mutations, more of a notice than a notion of defects.

He leaned into his chair and put his hands in back of his head, his elbows akimbo. "I'm glad for your company. I'm obliged to talk to the Bennies in the park soon."

June nodded. "I walked past the park this morning; that's why I came here. John said I should speak with you, perhaps even go with you."

"Bad?"

"Packed. And they're angry. The mayor is among them agitating. His office has set up food kiosks and porta-potties, so you know it's unpleasant just from that aspect." She paused. "It's that Drutz woman, the one who didn't care for Benny accommodations. Even in the clinic taking transfusions, she refused our food and water. She sent a Benny to the transit ship to get her fancy filtering water bottle and insisted he fill it up with the transit ship's water. She wouldn't eat anything I offered. It's Drutz who has the Bennies worked up with her promises."

June made a face and mocked Loren Drutz's voice. "Oh, Earth can't wait to welcome you home. We want to make it up to you. We'll fix whatever is wrong, give you money and new homes, blah, blah, blah."

"I know," Arlen said. "What a snake. We need to shove them off. Let them go back to Earth and get the big welcome. After all, they all have the antibodies, too." He turned to Howard. "How's the computer work going?"

"Great," Howard answered. "We know where the other Freak Ships are, and we have all the star chart computers. In fact, we only left the ship's homing apparatus so they can get back to Earth, but nowhere else."

June cocked her head. "No communication devices?"

"No," Howard said. "Arlen told us to take everything the day all of the crew came to the clinics in Benevolence. We have it all. We've been doing our research here, in the city."

"Well," June said, stroking her pleated chin. "If there weren't devices for communication, how could Loren Drutz have spoken with anyone on Earth? How could she have arranged all the welcome-home crap she's touting to the Bennies?"

Arlen looked away and back. "And Earth doesn't know about curing the plague either." He processed for a few moments. "She had no intention of telling the scientists on Earth about the antibodies. She would have kept Bennies and crew locked in the Monitor, and she would have used the capsule to return to Earth. There she'd make arrangements to keep captives. Like milking cows, only she would sell the antibody serum." He brought his hands down on the desktop. "I really need to see Max."

Samantha put her hand to her mouth. "General Keel?" She ran to her desk. "Lookie here, what I have. A Walkie-Talkie, compliments of the H W S. Monitor." Pressing the button on the device made a beep. "General Keel?" she said with a slight giggle, "Mr. Rowell wishes your presence, stat!"

While they waited for Max, Arlen asked Howard to describe what they'd learned from the computers.

Howard, a shy person, got excited. "We know where the other Freak Ships are located, and we know how to get there. Our FTL drives will be functional soon, too, maybe today. We've taken the capsules from the Monitor, so when we get within capsule range to the closest ship, the Comfort, we can dock and explain what has happened. Then we'll find the other ships, the Security, the Reverence, Mercy, the Veneration... here." He handed Arlen a list of all the names.

Arlen nodded. "If those other ships align with us, we can surely find a suitable planet. Fifty thousand is a good number for defense and to set down roots. With that many folks working together, there's no reason we can't make a new life on a habitable planet."

"Except for one thing, Arlen." June sighed. "We need to repopulate. I'm suspecting that whatever keeps us Bennies infertile has the same effect on the other Freak Ships."

Arlen looked at Howard. "Any evidence of why we can't reproduce?"

"Not that I've noticed, but I haven't been looking for reasons. My specialty is hacking computers, not science, or hormones, or whatever."

June put up her finger. "Wait a minute. Hormones?"

Arlen leaned toward her. "What are you thinking, June?"

"The transit ship brings us our protein powder, and we never know when it docks, right? What if, at the same time, they are salting our water supply with anti-fertility hormones?"

"Samantha," Arlen said. "Have Candy check the lists and see who has the background to look into that. He or she can work with Howard on the computers."

"Right, Boss. On it."

The room stayed silent until Samantha came back; this time, she had Max with her. She giggled when she announced him. "General Keel to see you, sir."

"Hey, Max," Arlen said.

"At your service, Commander-in-Chief." Max clicked his heels together smartly and saluted. Then he chuckled. "What can I do for you?"

"Is it possible to herd the Normals into the Monitor?"

"Done, with a guard at the portal."

Arlen turned to Howard. "Any chance we can remotely send them off?"

Howard thought for a few seconds. "I think so."

"Set it up." He looked at Max. "Do you think I need an armed guard to go to the park?"

"Oh, yeah. They're mad as hell. That Drutz woman left the Monitor when the guard took a pee break. She was at the park all afternoon yesterday until we marched her to the transit ship. It took four of us to surround her and make her go. You should have heard the Bennies. They called us all sorts of names. When you get there...well...it'll be interesting. I hope you have some proof that Drutz has given them the mickey."

"I have proof. Are you ready?"

"I'll go with you," June said.

"Me, too," Samantha added.

Howard stood up. "I'll go to the computer lab."

"Okay," Arlen said. "Stop at Candy's desk and see who she thinks you should work with on the fertility thing."

Max patted the plasma rifle slung over his shoulder. "Gertrude is ready. Let's go."

"Hey, Max," Arlen said, as he held the door for the ladies, "would it be safe to shoot Gertrude in Benevolence?"

"Hell, no. I hope I don't have to."

The four of them, Max and Samantha, plus Arlen and June, strode down the street. It wasn't a day like usual. People milled around the buildings, and store owners kept their doors shut. The feeling of expectation soaked the atmosphere.

"Edgy," Arlen told June. "Everyone is edgy."

"They don't know what will happen. They're watching you to see how you handle this problem."

"What if I fail?"

June's wrinkled cheeks bunched up in a smile. "You won't."

He believed her.

Sixteen

As they approached the park, they heard the hum of a large crowd and not a happy hum. When a few of the detainees recognized Arlen, they began to yell, and the echoes bouncing off the metallic sides and blue sky of Benevolence blended and swirled into a deafening roar.

Arlen put both arms up and shouted. "People!"

He waited until the noise abated. Anna Liza came to the periphery and glared at him. Standing in front of him was the woman he had loved, wanted to marry, and no longer respected or desired. He shook his head at her angry stare.

"People of Benevolence, you have been lied to by Loren Drutz."

The raving started anew. He waited.

June put up her hand and stepped in front of him. "Many of you know me. I wouldn't support our Liaison Officer, Arlen Rowell if I didn't know for certain that what he's telling you is true. You must listen."

The noise quieted.

"Thank you, June." He took a long look at this woman. She had saved his life, supported him, and recently discovered the proof he needed to address the crowd. And, she'd made it pretty clear she cared for him. His foolish sentiments for Anna Liza clouded what had been right before him. June.

He took a step, bringing him to her side. "Thank you, Junie." He added quietly, so only she could hear, "for everything."

She smiled. "Oh, you're welcome." The words said one thing, her face said, "finally."

"Bennies," Arlen began. "While the crew of the Monitor, including Loren Drutz, availed themselves of our services and life's blood, Howard Stadler and his men stripped the ship of their computers and communications devices. The crew, and Ms. Drutz, stayed in our clinics for two weeks, getting infusions. No communication left that ship at all, meaning Earth has not extended her welcome; has not promised you wealth and treatments for your mutations. Why do you need those things anyway? You have everything you need here. The mutations mean nothing here to your loved ones."

A bit of murmuring came from the crowd.

"Consider this. Why would Loren Drutz say those things and invite you to travel back to Earth when no one there knows about the cure or anything else? Are you thinking? She lied. She lied to get you in her grasp, where she would keep you captive and drain your blood for antibodies. Who do you think will get rich? Have fame? Have the glory for curing the new plague?"

People in the crowd talked to each other.

A messenger ran to Arlen. "Howard said he's found a way to remotely launch the Monitor. Does he have your permission?"

Arlen smiled wide. "Absolutely. No, wait." He put his hand up to address the crowd.

"We can launch the transit ship straight back

to Earth. The crew, including Ms. Drutz, possess your anti-bodies now. Let them be the lab rats for Humane Welfare. We have the capabilities to join the other Freak Ships. We'll invite the folks on those ships to come with us to search for a habitable planet, a new home. We can send off the old and head toward the new. What do you say?"

It took a few seconds, but the people in the crowd started cheering and got louder. Soon echoes bounced from their metallic city.

Arlen turned to the messenger. "Do it. And have Howard notify me the minute we have FTL. We can travel to the Comfort as soon as it's online."

Max called down the guards. Slowly the detainees dispersed.

"Mr. Rowell," a voice said behind Arlen. "You were and are correct."

"Thank you, Mayor Lewis. No hard feelings?"

"Yes. Of course, I have hard feelings. I knew someday one of you Liaisons would usurp my power."

Arlen folded his hands in front of his chest.

"Power? You know what? We're preparing to head out in space to link up with the other ships. Why don't you just take over all of this? I'll back off. You can deal with the other nine mayors or whatever government they have established. You can make all the decisions."

Lewis pulled at his half chin. "Nine ships? Hmm."

Arlen tapped his foot, waiting for the response.

"Nine ships, you say. Okay, this might be slightly out of my league. How about we work together? You behind the scenes, me doing what I always did. After all, I'm still mayor of Benevolence."

"Absolutely," Arlen said. "With all of the same power you always had." He kept his face taut to hide his real feelings.

Mayor Lewis smiled, turned away, and headed toward City Hall.

June looped her arm in his. "See. I said you wouldn't fail."

Arlen let out a long breath. "What will the Liaison Officer do now that we have divorced

Humane Welfare?"

"We don't need a Liaison Officer. We need a Commander-in-Chief. One who lets the mayor play mayor, of course. That, by the way, was a fine piece of finesse. God help us if you become a politician."

"Me? No way. Kick my ass if you see any of those signs from me."

"Gladly. Now, there's plenty to do. For one, we need to get on the infertility problem."

"Babies," Arlen said tenderly. "What would you think about having one?"

"I know how to get one, but with whom?" she said, faking coyness.

"With whom? Meem." He laughed. "As you can tell, I'm not so good with words."

"You did just fine a little while ago. Convinced a whole bunch of people to stand down with your words. Not to mention softening Lewis."

"Okay, with outraged people, I'm not so bad, but with a beautiful, intelligent, classy woman, I'm just a poor schlep."

"Spit it out, Arlen."

"Okay. Will you marry me?"

The pleats of her cheeks disappeared into each other from the wide smile. "Okay." Her eyes formed a question. "You feel confident we'll find a cure for the infertility?"

"I do."

She laughed. "I do. Too."

They walked silently back to the office.

When they arrived, Jeff Pendleton waited in Arlen's office.

"Uhm, hello…Jeff," Arlen said. His neck remembered vice grips.

"I'm sorry for what happened yesterday. I don't know what got into me."

"I do. The same thing that got into me. Luckily, we're both free from that influence. You are free of Anna Liza, right?"

Jeff nodded sadly.

"Don't worry about it. No problems. Be the bee's knees and keep us in green beans."

"That's not why I'm here," Jeff said. "Your clerk called me in. Something about hormones in the water, maybe?"

"You? Candy called you as the expert?"

"I am or was on Earth considered the expert on plant fertility. The way the hormones work is basically the same for all species when you get down to the nitty-gritty."

Of course. Mr. Wonderful. Eagle Scout, Ph.D. in what, everything? He wiped his face clear of scorn. "You could analyze our water to see if it has been treated?"

"I could. Why didn't I think of this before?"

Yeah, Super Bee, maybe you're not so smart. He glanced over at June. His Junie, who was so smart.

He nodded to Jeff. "Great, then. Analyze and let me know what you find out. And, Jeff, thanks. It's nice to have you on the team." Did he just say that? His neck wanted to know.

Jeff put out his baseball mitt hands to shake. Arlen placed his hand in the mitt and let Jeff close the sausages. Good enough.

After Jeff departed, he turned to June. "Don't you have work to do with Doctor Watson?"

"I was enjoying my engagement. But I guess I should leave. You might change your mind if I hang around."

"Not a chance." He pulled her close and kissed her. "Nice," he said. "Maybe we should shut the door and...."

"No way." She wiggled her left third finger. "Ring first." She cocked her head. "Just kidding about getting the ring first."

"Uhm, are there jewelers in Benevolence?"

"We can find rings. Not to worry. But seriously, Arlen, we both need to work. How about I fix dinner tonight at my place. Meatloaf. You bring the peanut butter."

Arlen laughed, kissed her again, and swatted her trim butt to send her off.

"What a day," he muttered. The Monitor had launched, the angry crowd had been placated, the FTL drives were almost ready, and he got engaged. Wow. He flipped through reports left by Howard outlining what they had discovered from the computers.

It took him hours to read all the reports, and at quitting time, when Candy, Ray, and Oscar left, Jeff returned.

"Found it. You were right. Humane Welfare has sterilized us with hormones in our water. I'll bet they introduced it each time they loaded our silos."

Arlen felt a wave of anger. He stifled it. "Do you think we've been affected permanently?"

"I'm not sure. But we need to get it out of our water supply right now before it has a chance to be permanent." He took a seat in front of the desk. "You know, we have all sorts of professions represented on Benevolence. But I've looked over the records, and no one on the list has experience with water filtration."

Arlen smiled. "No one on the list."

"No. The guys that diverted the sewage come the closest, but they aren't experts."

Arlen smiled again. "I am."

Jeff wrinkled his brow. "What?"

"High school dropout. But, having worked in my father's filtration business, I think I can step up to the plate."

"Unbelievable," Jeff said.

"That I'm smart enough to make special filters?"

"Oh, no. You're plenty smart. Have you ever heard the adage that when the student is ready, the teacher will come along?"

"Yeah, I've heard that."

Jeff stood and brushed lint off his trousers with his giant hands. "Have a good day." He waved with a baseball-mitt turn in the air and left.

Samantha hadn't gone home. She came into his office. "I stayed to give you this message."

He took the note and read it aloud. "FTL ready. Waiting for your okay to head for the Comfort."

Arlen leaned back in his office chair and smiled. "Give 'em the word to go."

She nodded, showed more teeth with her lipless smile, and withdrew, closing the door behind her.

He pushed the chair out a few inches, lifted his feet on his desk, and summoned the mental picture of drawings of a special filter he'd made with his father. As the lines appeared in his memory, he regretted the heartache he'd caused the man. He'd meant to apologize and reconnect, but his father had died days before Arlen was arrested for the shooting. He'd wanted his dad to be proud of him. Would helping fifty thousand people start a new life and be able to have children have made the old man proud? He sat up, drew the designs, and put notations next to the drawings. "For you, Dad," he whispered.

The light had dimmed to twilight when he headed home. He whistled as he walked. Here he was, saved from execution, living in a metal city that was soon to hurl faster than light through space to encounter another ship. He'd come through plague, fell out of love, and immediately back into it. He had become some kind of leader — commander-in-chief — of a group of people he admired. This evening he would dine with a beautiful, intelligent woman. And, soon, with his skills, he would give the lovers in Benevolence a chance at immortality through their offspring.

Wow. That's just the beginning of the adventure. What's going to happen when we rendezvous with the Comfort? And the other ships? Will we find a planet?" He stopped his mind from racing into the future and all the possibilities that waited.

He whistled a long, happy note. "Not bad for a twenty-eight-year-old drop-out." He thought.

"Not bad at all."

Patricia is a former art teacher and high school librarian. She lives in South Florida with her husband and three dogs. She writes short stories, novellas, and novels, mostly fantasy and Sci-Fi. She has also written three Romances, two Sci-Fi, a Victorian, and a Contemporary. Her stories revolve around action and deep relationships, allowing the reader to watch the scene unfold as if present. Patricia is active in three critique groups and often helps new writers learn the ropes. She is an active member of the Florida Writers Association, Mystery Writers of America, and Romance Writers of America.

When not writing, Patricia enjoys painting

watercolors and drawing in several media. Currently, she is learning illustration techniques for future books. Her frequent travel provides opportunities to check off bucket list items and sometimes inspires new stories. She is a voracious reader and loves a good book talk.

Check out her Facebook page at Carpewordum@ gate.net.